SILK

THE PRINCESS & THE SPY - PART 3

LISETTE MARSHALL

ISBN: 9789083256825

Cover design: 100Covers
Editor: Jennifer Lopez, Mistress Editing

www.lisettemarshall.com
www.facebook.com/LisetteMarshallAuthor
www.instagram.com/LisetteMarshallAuthor

CONTENTS

CONTENT NOTE

Silk deals with the death of a family member and portrays the grief and trauma of the surviving characters. The book contains some violence (not very graphic) and multiple sex scenes (graphic and fully consensual).

PROLOGUE

'Jaghar! The tower!'

Jaghar looked up from his saddle. Amidst the grey and brown of the mountains before them, it took him a moment to find the slightly different grey of Rock Hall's walls – but there it was indeed, the castle's main tower, looking out for them over the sharp edges of a nearby mountain.

A grin broke through on his face, fuelled in equal parts by the sight of home, the excitement in Velvet's voice, and perhaps the memories this specific part of the building evoked in him. Back at Rock Hall, after two months of absence. Longer than he had ever been gone since his first arrival at the castle – although somehow, in Velvet's company, it hadn't seemed even half as long.

'Can you imagine I'm even happier to see it than half a year ago?' she said.

Half a year ago. Her return from Copper Coast. Jaghar remembered, with amusing clarity, how irked he had been to see her upon that occasion, even as the picture-perfect fairy-tale princess she had pretended to be. And now... She looked nothing like that regal version of herself, in one of his shirts and boys' trousers they had bought along the way, tanned by weeks of riding in the late summer sun, her dark curls bound to the back of her head in a single messy bun. It had been a long time since he last thought of her as the crown princess of the Peaks. She was Velvet above all else to him now, his travelling companion for the past blissful weeks, his closest collaborator in the past blissful months.

His – wife-to-be? It still took an effort to believe it.

'In all modesty,' he said, 'I think you're speaking to the expert when it comes to being happier than half a year ago.'

She glanced over her shoulder at the road behind them, then leaned over, grabbed his hand, and pressed a quick kiss on his knuckles. The feeling of her lips against his skin lingered long after she let go of him and grabbed the reins again.

'Let's ride on, then.'

The roads grew more and more familiar as they crossed the last valleys and mountain ridges. None of the farmers and merchants they passed recognised them, and Jaghar could hardly blame them – a princess in boys' clothes and a smiling Spymaster? He might not have recognised himself a year ago.

'Velvet?'

'Hm?'

'Were you planning to change before we get there?'

'Oh, not really,' she said, turning to him with twinkling eyes. 'I think this will cause just the right amount of scandal to get people warmed up for all the outrageous things I'm about to do. Will be good for them.'

Jaghar grinned. 'I created a monster, didn't I?'

'Don't blame yourself. The monster largely created herself and is quite satisfied with the state of affairs.'

'I wouldn't dare to complain about lack of satisfaction, admittedly.'

They were still chuckling when they rode into town and began the final, steep ascent towards the gates of Rock Hall. None of their fellow travellers gave them as much as a glance even when they joined the queue of carts and horses at the gates of the castle, enjoying the summer sun while the merchants and guests were allowed inside one by one. A bored guard received them at the gate after some ten minutes of waiting, with an obligatory 'Name and reasons for—'

Only then did he abruptly swallow his words, squinting up at Velvet with a mixture of disbelief and growing concern.

'Dear gods – Your Highness?'

'Morning, Galen,' Velvet said with her most dazzling smile. 'Is my father at home?'

Trystan was at home, and came storming out of the castle in the least majestic outburst Jaghar had ever seen from him. 'Good gods, *Vivi*!'

'Father!'

She flew into his arms, crying and laughing at the same time. Around them, knights and nobles materialised out of nowhere within minutes, followed by a host of servants making good attempts to look like they had something urgent to do around the courtyard – dozens of eyes taking note of their princess as she reassured her father five, ten times that she *really* was healthy and happy and still fully alive. For the first time in his life, Jaghar couldn't be bothered to look cold and dangerous in full view of the court. A smile was creeping up on the corners of his mouth, and why in hell would he force it down again?

She was home. She was safe. She was his.

And judging by the look Trystan gave him when he eventually released his daughter, perhaps he wouldn't even need that much treason after all.

CHAPTER 1

Viviette woke up and needed a moment to understand where she was.

No grass. No trees. No gentle morning sun caressing her skin. Instead she found a familiar granite ceiling above her head, a tapestry depicting a lush green forest on her wall, a mess of warm furs and blankets around her body. Her own bed – it took her a moment too long. She was home again. She was *home*. And...

'Morning, Princess.'

She jolted up. Jaghar sat in his usual chair at the hearth, dressed already. His smile reminded her why she hadn't slept nearly as much as she should have, or why several parts of her body felt unusually sore even on her soft silk sheets.

'Good gods – you're not coming back for more, I hope?'

He raised an amused eyebrow. 'Complaints?'

'I'll be happy if I can sit down without flinching today,' Viviette said with a bright grin in his direction. 'And I'm pretty sure I need a bath, too. Anyway...'

'Apologies for disturbing you, then,' he said dryly. 'In that case I'll just go see your father on my own – let me know if you need company in that bath after...'

'Wait, wait – my father?'

He looked even more amused. 'He wanted to meet with me and Madelena to discuss the developments during our absence. Some updates about Donovan's recent actions, too. Thought you'd like to be there.'

Viviette blinked. 'Did he *ask* for me to be there?'

'Not at all, but as far as I'm concerned, that's his problem to solve, not yours.'

She sat up with a breathless laugh and winced as her weight landed on her rather sensitive bottom. 'I'll go dress myself.'

'A pity,' he said, 'but perhaps the best choice for the occasion indeed.'

She had trouble keeping her hands off him as they walked to her father's study together – after all these weeks of unsupervised travelling, with no-one but the trees and the hills to keep an eye on them, it was nearly a reflex to grab for his hand or to stop him for a kiss every other minute. Here...

She'd have to tell her father sooner or later, of course, but it seemed wiser to give the matter some time in at least the first weeks after their return.

Jaghar knocked when they reached the study, opened the door when her father's voice yelled an answer, and gestured her to go first. Viviette couldn't help but smile at the sight of the twinkle in his eyes. No need to keep acting all cold and distant towards each other, they had decided too. After weeks on the road, the court could assume they had at least stopped hating each other from the bottoms of their hearts.

At the desk inside, her father looked up, then froze and blinked in obvious confusion. In one of his guest chairs, Madelena looked unfazed as always.

'Good morning, Your Highness. Morning, Jaghar.'

'Morning,' he said dryly, closing the door. 'I brought a guest. Hope you don't mind – do we have chairs enough?'

'Plenty,' Viviette said cheerfully, falling into the chair next to Madelena and cowering as she hit the hard wooden seat. Her father was still visibly trying to make sense of her presence. Why hadn't she done this earlier, walk in and demand her place at the table? It turned out to be so easy... 'Good morning, Father.'

'Vivi? What in the world...'

'I understood you were going to discuss a few interesting subjects.' She smiled. 'So I thought I might as well come along.'

'But...' Her explanation only seemed to cause more confusion, or at least her father's glance at Jaghar

7

looked all but reassured. 'The reports of Donovan's recent activities might be a little upsetting. I don't want to—'

'Finding his wife in his bedroom was also quite upsetting,' Viviette interrupted. 'I seem to have survived that too. Also, I'm not planning to let the bastard surprise me a second time, so if you don't mind, I'll just stay here and listen to the news. I doubt I'll faint.'

Jaghar sank down in the last free chair and gave her father an apologetic shrug. 'More or less my thoughts.'

'You could have asked...'

'You'd have said no,' Viviette said, and her father stared at her, then at Jaghar, and back at her again. Next to her, Madelena sat up straighter, a suspicious smile on her face.

'Since Her Highness does indeed not give the impression she's about to faint, I suggest we simply get to work, Your Majesty?'

Her father opened his mouth, but let out a slightly bewildered sigh without objecting. 'I – well, yes, let's start. Vivi, if at any point you'd rather leave...'

'I'll warn you if I get the vapours, yes.'

Jaghar was quite obviously suppressing a grin. Viviette thought it wiser to avoid his eyes, fearing she might burst out in a hysterical fit of laughter if she actually looked at him. Her father seemed puzzled enough as it stood.

'Wonderful,' Madelena said, grabbing a pile of notes from the desk before her. 'So, to begin with the most relevant part – Donovan.'

'Hasn't been sitting back idly, I suppose?' Jaghar said, raising an eyebrow.

'Not quite, no. That is to say – Your Highness, the news of your disappearance of course made the rounds rather quickly, together with the news that Ysabel was on her way to Whitemarsh again. Most people were able to see the link and get at least some rudimentary idea of what happened, which – well, at my last count four of Donovan's dukes were making noise to dethrone him altogether. Some others are lobbying to at least send someone in his place at the next royal summit of the Five Kingdoms. Especially those on the border with the Lower Riverlands would rather not put him around the table with Emrys at the next meeting of kings.'

Viviette barely suppressed a smile. Internal unrest was not the violent death Donovan deserved, in her opinion, but at least it was a fine step in the right direction.

'The problem is,' her father said slowly, 'that all this turmoil forced Donovan to come up with a different story. He's now spreading the tale that Ysabel faked her *own* death in order to run away with some lover.'

'What in the world?'

'That she lied to you when you found out about her existence, Vivi. That she set you up against Donovan, and that you returned to Rock Hall too quickly for him to explain himself to you.'

Viviette stared at him. His green eyes stood tired, but he seemed fully earnest.

'A rather worthless story, isn't it?' she said.

9

'Of course it is,' her father said with a feeble smile. 'But people who don't know the details you wrote about – the locked door of her room and Cillian's – well, behaviour – might as well believe it. In the end, it's your word against Donovan's.'

'Emrys will never believe this story either. And I doubt Tamar will be fooled.'

'Donovan probably hopes that we'll realise how much we need him. If he can get his internal troubles under control – well, the other kingdoms will have to make a decision. The Taavi are still lurking around the borders, and it won't help to drive Donovan into their arms.'

'After the Empress tried to kill his betrothed on the road?' Jaghar said wryly. 'Suppose his nobles will have something to say about that too.'

'The Empress sticks to the story that she had nothing to do with that attack. Highwaymen gone rogue, according to her account. If Donovan is clinging to lies anyway, he might as well accept this one too. Which means he may well look for her help, unless...'

He didn't finish his sentence, with a quick look at Viviette. She read the rest of his words in the tension around his eyes – unless they continued to act as though nothing ever happened. Kept the alliance of the Five Kingdoms alive for the sake of peace, continued to welcome the bastard at the yearly gathering of kings and queens. Her throat tightened at the idea alone – the thought of her father still sitting around the same table with the man who had planned to use her as a present for his friends, the man who had locked his wife in lonely detention for two years...

But she ought to be reasonable now. Yes, Donovan deserved to drop to death from his own towers, but the people of the Five Kingdoms hadn't done anything to deserve the same fate. Handing the Taavi Empress a new ally, right between the other Kingdoms, was a risk they could take only in the direst circumstances. Did personal aversion really justify that step?

'I suppose it might be best to keep things civil, if he manages to keep his dukes from revolting,' she said slowly. 'Then again...'

'There's of course no reason we can't nudge those dukes towards revolt a little,' Jaghar finished next to her.

'Just what I was thinking.'

Her father frowned at her with obvious surprise – because of the suggestion or because of her sudden unanimity with Jaghar, she couldn't tell. 'Well – yes, that could certainly be a strategy, although there are of course some risks...'

'I'd see how the situation develops in the weeks to come,' Jaghar said. 'It will probably become clear what opportunities we have. As long as we can agree that the princess is not under any circumstances going back to the Riverlands?'

'We agree on that point,' her father said immediately, and a tension Viviette hadn't even known to exist melted off her shoulders.

'Wonderful,' she said dryly. 'But please keep me informed about the rest as well. Any other recent developments I should know about?'

'Well.' Her father cleared his throat. 'This is perhaps not a matter to discuss so soon, but if you want to be fully informed – Ulrick wrote me last week to rather unsubtly remind me that you have known his stepson for a long time, and that in case you're looking to rekindle an old friendship...'

'Oh, the vultures are gathering around the loot already?'

'Vivi!'

She snorted. 'Good gods, Father. The deplorable timing aside – does Ulrick really believe it's anything of a commendation that I've known Roark for a long time? I know he's a violent, unmannered jerk with no other passions than killing things, yes. I'd throw myself into the abyss before I'd marry him.'

'Vivi...'

'I'm not marrying anyone now.' She hadn't planned to broach the subject today, but her careful planning was worthless in the face of her fury – at her father for even considering the option more than at Ulrick for suggesting it. 'If anyone writes you any such thing again, please tell them I'm not available – or don't, but then I'll take it upon myself, and your wording will likely be more polite.'

Her father opened his mouth, then abruptly turned to Jaghar. 'Do you have any opinions?'

'Me?' Jaghar said, raising an eyebrow. 'I'm not sure why you'd ask me, in all honesty. Unless you believe Roark might accept me as a sufficient alternative for the princess, I don't see what my preferences have to do with the matter.'

Viviette accidentally snorted out loud, and Jaghar's quick grin in her direction didn't help to keep her laughter under control either. Her father's eyes shot back and forth between the two of them, his frown deepening with every turn.

'Perhaps this is again a matter for another moment?' Madelena suggested, still thoroughly unperturbed. 'We have a rather lengthy list of smaller developments throughout the Kingdoms and the Empire to discuss, which—'

'Yes, yes,' her father interrupted without looking at her. 'Of course, Jaghar, there is a lot you need to be informed about. Vivi...' He seemed to have trouble getting his words in line. 'Vivi, could we have a word in private? Unless you want to hear every detail Madelena and Jaghar have to consider...'

'Oh – no, I don't suppose so.' She would get the important news anyway. 'Do you want to speak with me now?'

'Yes, please – Jaghar, Madelena, my apologies. Hope it's not an inconvenience.'

'Not at all,' Madelena said lightly, gathering her notes and files. 'Shall we move to the office, Jaghar?'

'Yes.' He hesitated for a moment, then gave Viviette a quick glance, one eyebrow raised. She flashed a smile with a little more confidence than she felt. She shouldn't have been so direct so quickly, of course, now who knew what her father might say – but then again, it wouldn't help anyone if Jaghar got himself involved in the fight as well.

He nodded and stood up without another word, turning towards her father. 'I'll see you after diner to discuss the rest, then?'

'Yes. Thank you, Jaghar.'

Then they were gone, leaving the study in a tense, expectational silence broken only by the shouts of practicing knights outside. Viviette waited. After what felt like hours, her father cleared his throat.

'Vivi, of course I understand that after all you've been through another engagement is the last thing you're looking for...'

'But you need me to marry to make sure Emeric's treacherous shoulders don't end up under the silk cloak?' she finished laconically, and he blinked again.

'Well – I suppose that is about the gist of it. Which means—'

'It doesn't really mean much, Father.'

'Vivi—'

'No, wait – let me finish, will you?' She took a deep breath, bracing herself. Fine, then. Perhaps it was best to have it behind her as fast as possible. 'That whole issue with Emeric shouldn't matter at all. You have the power to simply name me your heir, marriage or not. So why exactly are you so desperate to get me a husband, then?'

He didn't avert his eyes, but he didn't answer either. Viviette leaned back in her chair and folded her arms, forcing the next sentence from her lips.

'Because if I'm very honest, it looks like you simply don't trust me to do this on my own.'

'That...'

He didn't finish his sentence, leaving an even heavier silence in its wake. Viviette didn't speak until he looked away and sank back in his chair, his lips clenched so tightly the skin paled around them.

'You always told me you were trying to protect me,' she said. The words came out strangely cold – a hard, sharp certainty, far beyond the flaming anger Ulrick's suggestions evoked in her. 'But it never kept me out of danger. All it did was keep me ignorant of what was going on. You could have prepared me. You could have taught me how to do this on my own. And instead you'd rather chain me into some unhappy marriage that will force me to look on while my husband is doing the things I want to do myself?'

'Vivi, I—'

'I know you meant well. I know you don't want to hurt me. But I deserve better than this, Father. *I* know I'm better than this. I'm not going to be some decorative accessory for the rest of my life.'

'I never intended you to be.'

'What other fate did you prepare me for, exactly?'

He closed his eyes. 'I'm looking to find you a reliable husband, Vivi, someone who—'

'Someone who doesn't see his wife as a pretty toy?'
She uttered a sharp laugh. 'I think we learned that it's
hard to be certain of anyone's intentions in this world.
I'm not placing my faith in them, at least.'

He remained silent. She swallowed her nervousness
down.

'So as far as I can see there are three options. Either
you try to marry me off anyway, at which I'll run
away and leave the throne to Emeric, or you don't
make me marry at all, in which case the throne will
again fall to Emeric, or you make me your heir with no
further conditions. In which case I can choose my own
husband. In which case I can divorce my own husband
if he turns out to be another monster, too.'

Her father didn't react. Behind him, a tapestry
fluttered – did the hidden door stand open? Was Jaghar
listening along? She could hardly blame him, and yet
her breath caught in her throat for an instant.

'Father?'

He stood, pacing to the window without looking at
her. 'You've never been so – when did you suddenly...'

'It didn't happen suddenly. You just didn't notice it
happening.'

'I...' He turned towards her, with an exasperated
gesture. 'Vivi, I just didn't want to bother you with...'

'Yes, and *I* want you to bother me with all of it. I can
handle it, Father. I've been listening along with you and
taking note of what you're doing for much longer than
you realise. I've handled poisonings and monstrous
husbands and weeks of fleeing through foreign lands –

I'll damn well handle a kingdom too. But you have to give me the chance to do it.'

With a muffled curse he leaned back against the windowsill and rubbed his eyes. For a moment they were both silent.

Then he slowly said, 'And if I were to make you my heir – if you were to choose your own husband – do you by any chance – happen to have an idea already...'

He didn't finish his question. Viviette stared at him, the silence burning on her tongue. She didn't want to lie. She really, really didn't want to lie. But if she told him – if he'd disagree – all chances would have vanished at once.

'Perhaps that's not a question I should ask now,' he added, more quietly. 'From the perspective of trusting you.'

'No.' She hesitated. 'Father, I won't be stupid, I promise. I'll find someone who understands politics, someone who can keep the Peaks safe – but I want it to be my choice. If you can't trust me on that, you should go find another heir.'

'I – I have no intentions to go find another heir, Vivi.'

She barely dared to breathe, staring at him as he stared at the floor, his green eyes tired and pensive. A hope she had never truly allowed herself to feel came seeping through now, filled her with a strange, expectant lightness – *no intentions*. Which seemed to mean...

'I'll have to arrange a number of things,' he said, looking up. 'I can't take a decision like this without discussing it with a number of people first – my advisors, our more powerful dukes – if they have any serious reasons to disagree, I'll have to seek a solution to their objections first.'

'But you *will*...'

'Yes.'

'You – Father!' Tears stung behind her eyes. 'I – oh, gods, I hadn't thought...'

He stepped around his desk and spread his arms. Viviette jumped up from her seat and fell into his embrace, clenching her arms around him as if she were five years old again and had stumbled and scraped her knee – a warm, safe hug like when he had still been infallible in her eyes. His voice sounded somewhat smothered next to her ear.

'I'm sorry, Vivi. I'll try to do you justice from now on.'

She nodded wordlessly against his shoulder, blinking back tears. Her father's arms only held her tighter.

His heir.

He would name her his *heir*.

Even now the triumph wouldn't come through entirely yet, the full realisation of the consequences. She would never see Donovan again. Her father wouldn't marry her to Roark, or anyone else. *She* could choose...

Jaghar. Oh, bless the gods – *Jaghar*.

'I have to go see some people now,' he said eventually. 'Take some time to recover from your long journey, I'd say. If you want to know all I'm doing, you'll be busy enough very soon.'

Viviette laughed. 'You're not deterring me.'

'I wouldn't dare.' He smiled at her. 'We'll talk soon, alright?'

She nodded and turned around, suppressing the urge to skip towards the door. Behind her, her father said, 'Oh, and Vivi?'

'Yes?'

'Did you speak with Jaghar about this?'

She froze mid-step. 'Why would you think...'

He sank down in his chair, tilting his head in an uncomfortably interested gesture. 'Just – out of curiosity. You get along better than you did before, don't you?'

'Oh.' She opened her mouth, and hesitated. 'Well. I suppose – if someone saves your life – and then continues to keep you alive for weeks – it's rather hard to keep believing he's a jerk. So I suppose I've – quite grown to appreciate him, yes.'

'I'm glad to hear, Vivi.' There was something uneasily satisfied about his smile; for a moment he strangely resembled the old ladies in Copper Coast who spent their days cooking up promising matches between their pupils. 'I'm – very, very glad to hear.'

She didn't manage to get a hold of Jaghar for the rest of the day, while Madelena was burying him under the details of everything that had happened in Rock Hall and the Five Kingdoms for the past several weeks. But when he stepped into the dinner hall that evening and met her gaze, she knew he had already heard the news of her father's decision. Even in full view of the court, something suspiciously close to a smile hovered around his lips – a smile that made her heart melt a little every time she glanced at him during the meal. She'd seen it before in the past weeks, lingering on his face whenever he thought she wasn't looking at him – and somehow the sight of his quiet happiness made her even happier than the prospect of marrying him itself.

She knew he was still keeping an eye on her when she wandered out into the gardens after dinner. He found her between the flower beds minutes later, scaring away the young ladies who had followed her outside with a single, well-aimed glare. Viviette barely suppressed her laughter until they had scurried out of hearing distance.

'Evening, Spymaster.'

'Evening, Your Majesty.'

Her smile grew broader. 'That's assuming everything goes according to plan.'

'I know your father a little, Velvet. Some grumbling dukes aren't going to change his mind.'

'I hope not.' She glanced over her shoulder. A few dinner guests were eyeing them, doubtlessly hoping to catch some juicy gossip after her recent return – but nobody stood close enough to hear their conversation. 'I wanted to ask you – perhaps I'm getting unreasonably suspicious about everything, but is it possible he suspects something?'

Jaghar raised an eyebrow. 'The king?'

'Yes? He – wait, did you listen along?'

'He asked for private conversation with you,' he said dryly. 'I have some decency left.'

Viviette grinned. 'My apologies – I thought I saw something move behind the tapestries, but perhaps it was the draught. In any case, he asked about you. That is to say, he asked if we spoke about this, and I told him I didn't quite hate you anymore. He said he was very, *very* happy to hear. Looked unusually satisfied, too.'

Jaghar blinked, then turned away, focussing on the mountain tops before them with glassy, dark eyes. 'Do you think...'

'I have no idea. I mean, he didn't *say* anything. But after that conversation, asking about you just seemed... suggestive?'

She watched him wrestle with his thoughts for a moment – as she had seen him do so often whenever she told him anything that didn't align with the stories he told himself, the man he thought himself to be. It looked too good to be true, of course, her father happily agreeing with their plans – but after a long afternoon of deliberation, it didn't even seem that mad anymore. He *did* trust Jaghar, after all. He *did* consider him a good man. He knew the Peaks would be safe in his hands. It didn't strengthen any alliances, admittedly, but then again, at least this marriage couldn't ruin any alliances either if it turned out her prospective husband was not who he appeared to be...

'Only makes me feel more ashamed to lie to him,' Jaghar muttered.

'We could tell him.'

The words left her lips before she could think them through – words she'd never even have come up with if not for that meaningful smile on her father's face that morning. Tell him. A ridiculous idea, of course, and yet...

She didn't want to lie. She didn't want to wait. She didn't want to pretend for years to come.

'I'm not sure whether you're insane or brilliant, Velvet.'

She managed a laugh. 'Both, possibly. I mean, it's a risk. But we don't need to tell him about the time before Donovan – we could just say – you know, weeks of travelling together...'

'Yes.' He pressed his lips. 'I suppose that doesn't sound too ridiculous.'

'No more ridiculous than me ordering you to take my virginity because I wanted to join some masked brothel,' Viviette said dryly, and he grinned.

'You're making a fair point there.'

'Thanks. But in all earnestness, he might be angry, or he might as well be relieved I'm not running of with some brainless Copper Coast count. Perhaps the latter is slightly more likely.'

An absent shadow slid over his face. Then, abruptly, he turned around and held out his arm, his raised eyebrow something in between an invitation and a challenge.

'Are you coming, then?'

'What – now?'

'I'm seeing him anyway.'

SILK

She opened her mouth and closed it again. Now? *Now*? That inviting arm alone... She had never held him or barely even touched him in public. Rumours might buzz through Rock Hall before they even reached her father's room, and then what in the world was she going to do if he forbade them to ever see each other again?

But he had smiled, this afternoon. That gentle, satisfied smile...

She laid her hand on Jaghar's dark sleeve in a surge of courage. Her heart slammed into her throat the same moment.

'We're going mad, aren't we?'

He laughed, leading her back inside the castle. She barely dared to look at him, with her heart pounding in her chest so violently that her thoughts turned dizzy – telling him. *Telling* him. So many hours spent hiding the truth from her father, and now a single smile and one impulsive suggestion were enough to change everything – if only he wouldn't be angry, if only he'd agree, she could as well be openly in love tomorrow morning... The castle was turning around her as they crossed the hall and climbed the stairs. Please, *please* don't let him be angry...

The sharp sound of Jaghar's knuckles against the study door shook the world back into place. Now finally she dared to meet his eyes. The tension was all too visible on his face, but something strangely calm lay in his look as well. No turning back, she knew at that moment. Not if she wanted to free him from that continuous guilt gnawing at him.

Her father's room remained silent. Jaghar raised an eyebrow and knocked again, then simply opened the door when an answer again failed to come out.

He froze.

He froze in exactly the wrong way, his breath catching in his throat, his eyes widening at something inside Viviette was unable to see.

'Jaghar?'

'No.' He pushed her back the moment she stepped towards the room; his free hand shot to the knife at his belt. His voice was too sharp. 'No. Stay there, Velvet. You – you don't want to see—'

'What in the world—'

'Stay *there*!'

Panic cracked through his voice. That, more than anything, shut down every muscle in her body for a heartbeat – Jaghar, panicking. His heavy breath. His fingers, trembling when he grabbed her arm to shove her out of the way.

'What in the world...'

'Your father. Your father – gods, Velvet...' His voice broke. 'He – he's dead?'

CHAPTER 2

The castle had gone eerily quiet when Jaghar stepped through the study door again an hour later, his thoughts numb, his limbs stiff with shock. Even knowing what awaited him, his eyes were barely able to focus on the scene before him.

Trystan's body.

Thrown over his desk like he had fallen asleep in his chair. Right hand still holding his pen. Left hand clawing into a pile of parchment. Green eyes wide in an expression of terror that Jaghar had never wanted to see on this face.

A knife hilt sticking out between the shoulder blades, the blue silk around it drenched in blood.

Nothing about the scene felt real. It simply didn't make sense. Hours ago Trystan had still been a walking, speaking, smiling man. How could that same man suddenly no longer exist? Staring at the dead face before him, Jaghar was overcome by a strange, desperate certainty that that bloodied knife was only a temporal issue – that any moment the king would sit up and shake the blade from his back, smile his familiar, gentle smile, and reassure him that of course the injury was not nearly so severe at all...

But the body before him remained empty and motionless, a shell devoid of all signs of life.

'Spymaster?'

Sir Bertram appeared in the doorway behind him, his gruff voice unusually quiet. Jaghar jolted around and tried to scrape himself together – he had to be in control now, like he was always in control when the rest of the world fell apart...

But his thoughts were reeling, unable to grasp the fact that this evening was truly happening, that he wasn't wandering through some cruel and elaborate dream from which he could wake any moment.

'Has Emeric been informed?' he managed. That, he vaguely recalled, was something he had mentioned somewhere in the past hour.

'He has been, yes.'

'Everybody is being kept in their rooms? Servants gathered in the hall? Nobody allowed in and out of the castle?'

'Yes.' Bertram coughed. 'Prince Emeric suggested to write the dukes of the Council. He is taking care of it at this very moment, I believe.'

The Council. The seven dukes of the Peaks who were to confirm Trystan's successor in three nights. Rarely more than a formality – yet this time...

Jaghar closed his eyes, forcing his breath to slow. His thoughts felt too dull, too heavy, as if wading through sticky mud. They couldn't appoint Emeric. They wouldn't appoint Emeric. He'd rather kill the bastard than allow him to wear the silk cloak Trystan had tried to keep out of his hands. But if the Council didn't know the king's decision of mere hours ago...

Bertram cleared his throat behind him. 'Spymaster?'

'Yes – yes, very well.' His disoriented thoughts were seeping through his mask at all sides, and he didn't manage to stop them. What in the world did it matter if he failed? Trystan wouldn't be here to congratulate him on his work. Trystan would never congratulate him on anything again. 'Is there anything else we need to arrange tonight? Has the king's secretary been informed?'

'Lord Reginald is aware and looking at the administrative matters.' Bertram hesitated. 'Do you know where the princess is?'

'The princess is safe.' He had left her in Madelena's care – he couldn't subject her to the hysteria of courtly ladies while he was arranging the castle's safety measures and setting investigations in motion. 'I'll go see her in a minute.'

'I see. In that case...'

They were both silent for the moment. Then Bertram again cleared his throat and continued, with audible trouble, 'We'll – have to find out who did this, Spymaster.'

'Yes.'

'Are you...'

'I'll get to work in a moment.'

'Is there – is there anything else I can do?'

'No,' Jaghar said, closing his eyes. 'To tell you the truth, I think there isn't. Keep everybody in their place. Make sure nobody starts panicking and nobody else is killed. I'll let you know if anything else needs to be done.'

Bertram sighed, his shoulders sagging as his gaze moved to Trystan's body for the shortest moment. 'As you wish.'

'Thank you.'

The door shut softly behind him. In the corridor, the heavy footsteps of metal-plated boots removed themselves just too slowly.

Jaghar sank down on the floor, his knees giving in as the weight of watching eyes was lifted off his shoulders for the first time since the discovery of the body. An investigation. The first of his duties now, he was aware. But the idea alone seemed futile and pathetic. What in the world would it help to investigate *now*, after the unthinkable had already happened? Demon be damned, why hadn't he gone here directly after dinner? Why hadn't he been in this very room to stop the attacker? Why had he thought he could stay down in that garden for so long?

An hour ago the world had still been about to turn into paradise. Velvet at his arm. Trystan's cryptic approval. And now?

'What in the world are we going to do, King?' he whispered.

A dead, cold silence. The glassy green eyes didn't come alive.

'Please.' Useless. Pointless. 'You can't leave me here like this. You can't just – stop existing. I need you. The Peaks need you. Velvet...'

His voice broke. The memory of her trembling body under his hands, her blank, terrified eyes following him as he walked out of Madelena's room...

'I'm sorry,' he managed to the motionless body before him. A pressure was building up behind his eyes, like a stinging headache – but he hadn't cried for decades, and the tears couldn't find their way outside even now. 'I'm so sorry. I should never have lied to you. I just – love her more than anything I've ever loved in the world – but I wanted to tell you the truth one day, I swear I wanted to...'

Outside the room, far away, a woman's voice wailed and cried. Here inside not even the curtains moved. Jaghar closed his eyes. He's gone, he tried to tell himself. It doesn't matter what you say – he won't hear you. He's not coming back. He can't help you. But every thought felt like a scorching lie, and when he looked up and found the body hadn't moved, his heart shattered in his chest all over again.

'I – I suppose I have to investigate this,' he said, numbly. 'I have to find out who did this to you. I'll find out, I promise – even if it's the last thing to do, I will solve it. I'll do what you wanted me to do – keep the Peaks safe. Keep your daughter safe.'

Velvet. Who should be the next queen. Who would have to carry the weight of her kingdom on her frail shoulders too soon, and too suddenly.

Someone would have to help her.

Abruptly the strength returned to his limbs. He scrambled back to his feet, his blood rushing through him again, his thoughts clearing up a little – this, finally, was an order even his paralysed heart could understand. Keep her safe. He shouldn't be sitting here talking to the dead. He should be by her side, carrying her through these days, and through the rest of her life if need be.

'I'll make sure she'll get through,' he muttered, lowering his head and turning for the door. 'I'll make sure she's loved.'

The world fell away around him when he opened the door of Madelena's office and found Velvet curled up in a chair. For a single, unmoving moment her slender body was all he saw, arms wrapped around herself, head lowered in quiet despair; then she noticed him and jolted up, her green eyes widening in sudden relief.

'Jaghar! Thank the gods...'

He had his arms around her before he could think twice about it, lowered his face into her dark curls and pressed her against him. Her fingers clawing into his back were the first thing that pulled him back into reality, back into the bitter truth of this incomprehensible night. Trystan was gone – truly, definitively gone – but she was still here, and he still loved her to death, and at least that was one certainty in the world he could cling to...

'Something to drink?' Madelena's pragmatic voice broke through their embrace.

Jaghar looked up. She stood in the corner of the room, a teapot in her hands and a mismatched collection of crystal glasses and earthenware mugs on the side table next to her. Her eyes stood unusually tired, but the faint smile on her face was still as incorruptible as always – a smile that quite emphatically realised he was clutching a princess against his chest, that he had all but kissed the crown of that same princess's head moments before, and that he had no decent reason to be doing either. But Velvet didn't pull away from him, and his arms refused to let go of her.

'Do you have anything stronger?' he said.

Madelena pulled a crystal carafe from the mantlepiece without further comments and poured him a generous glass of a deep golden liquor. He averted his face and laid a hand around the back of Velvet's head, holding her against his shoulder. A warmth was spreading through him from the places where their bodies were pressed together, a mortifying arousal tugging at the last steely self-restraint that kept him together – not now, he tried to convince his own body, not this evening from hell, but his mind was clinging to anything other than death, and nothing was life like the way she made his blood flow...

Madelena put his glass down on the desk with a louder thud than necessary. Velvet jolted and pulled free from his embrace, looking neither of them in the eyes as she sank back into her chair and folded her knees to her chest again.

'Jaghar?' Madelena said.

He turned to her, desperately trying to dissuade the rush of blood to his loins. She was looking from Velvet to him, her eyebrows raised in a cartload of justified suspicion.

'Hm?' he said.

'How long has this been going on?'

He couldn't bring up the energy to lie. 'Couple of months.'

'Ah.' She seemed hardly surprised. 'Explains a thing or two. Take a seat. You can't keep standing there for the rest of the night.'

He had always found her resolute calm a blessing when it came to dealing with troublesome clients or incoherent witnesses. Never before had he realised she would keep her head together even when he couldn't. He sank down in the chair next to Velvet without thinking any further and gulped down a third of his glass at once. At least the liquor burning through his throat assured him that he was still more or less awake and alive. At least it moved his thoughts away from Velvet's fragile beauty and Trystan's lifeless body for a moment.

Madelena sat down as well and wiped her blonde curls from her face. 'So, what's the state of affairs?'

'Castle is locked down,' Jaghar said, closing his eyes. The image of the knife in Trystan's back still stuck to his mind's eye. He didn't want to be reasonable now. He wanted to scream, and punch something, and lose himself fucking someone – but a hard, cold wall held him back, numbing everything he said and did. 'Vander is checking the list of people who were seen around the study after dinner. Branwen is looking if there's anyone in Rock Hall who shouldn't have been here in the first place – although I must say it seems unlikely that we'll find the solution in a stranger.'

'How so?'

'Someone stabbed him in the back while he was working,' Velvet said before Jaghar could answer. Her voice sounded dull, and she didn't lift her head from her knees. 'He must have been busy while someone else was walking through the study. He'd never let strangers pace around without keeping an eye on them.'

A flare of admiration tore through him, mingling with his sickening arousal. 'Exactly.'

'Ah.' Madelena's quick, surprised glance at Velvet didn't escape him. 'Fair point. That should quite narrow down our pool of suspects.'

'Yes,' Jaghar said curtly. 'It still leaves the question *why* anyone would suddenly decide they wanted him dead, though.'

'Do you think...' Velvet looked up, her voice higher now. 'Do you think it may have anything to do with – me?'

'I don't see how it could.' He rubbed his eyes. Please, don't let it have anything to do with her. 'The timing is suspicious, but hardly anyone even knew about the plan – only Madelena, Reginald and me, and I don't think Reginald knows how to use a knife. So there might be something else going on.'

'Oh, I could think of a few people who'll be happier than they should be when they get this news,' Madelena said gloomily. 'Our old friend Osric – the one who's probably smuggling diamonds over the Taavi border – may now avoid his court case after all—'

'Osric is on the Council, too,' Velvet interrupted her.

'He is, yes – that might be an additional complication. Then there's the High Priest – I told you about that issue, didn't I, Jaghar?'

Velvet frowned. 'Hamond? What's the matter with him?'

'Has been fondling Temple virgins during the ritual of the midnight fire,' Jaghar said grimly. 'For years, apparently.'

'What?'

34

Madelena sighed. 'We only found out last week –
one of the girls told a friend who happened to be the
sister of one of our men. I told the king, and some
of our people have been asking around in the Temple
since. *If* Hamond caught air of that investigation...'
She shook her head. 'He might have been desperate
enough. People have been executed for defamation of
the Temple.'

'Oh, gods.'

'Yes.' Madelena threw Jaghar a quick glance. 'And
there are some other options too – I don't know
whether you consider it likely that the Taavi have taken
up on their old strategies again?'

'Could be, in theory,' he said, ignoring the old,
familiar pang of pain. 'They'd prefer Emeric as king
of the Peaks, at least. But on the other hand, I don't
see why they'd need Emeric *now*, and...' He paused. 'It
doesn't seem like their style.'

'In what way?'

'The Taavi generally plan their murders. This looks
more like a spontaneous attack – nobody could have
known...'

Madelena picked up on his hesitation immediately.
'The planning was that you'd be with the king directly
after dinner, wasn't it?'

He closed his eyes, his guts cramping up. Trystan had
probably not even bothered to keep his guards around
in those few minutes. If he had been a little earlier – if
he hadn't ignored his duty for a few minutes too long,

hadn't wasted so much time entertaining himself in that damned garden...

Next to him, Velvet didn't speak, and the silence hurt more than his own thoughts. Madelena nodded slowly.

'Admittedly – and Donovan?'

Velvet stiffened up beside him. 'Donovan?'

'I suppose you two are quite a threat to him at this moment, at least,' Madelena said, with a glance aside. 'You know what he did to Ysabel. He presumably knows the king would believe you and might cause him trouble. Is it possible that he sent someone?'

Velvet swallowed, the knuckles of her fists paling. 'I – I wouldn't see it beyond him, I think.'

Jaghar averted his eyes, his heart pounding in his ears. The memory of Ysabel's ordeal and that horrific scene in Donovan's study were bad enough already; the idea that the same bastard could be responsible for Trystan's death...

'I'll make sure we have a word with all visitors from the Higher Riverlands,' Madelena said, pulling an empty sheet of parchment from one of the piles on her desk to jot down a list. 'And perhaps I'll advertise the service a little in those circles. Paulette is seeing Osric tonight, so we can see whether anything sensible comes from that side. And as to Hamond...' She shook her head. 'We don't have any eyes in the Temple at this moment. I can introduce someone, but it may take a few days.'

A few days. In three nights the Council would come together and crown the next king or queen of the Peaks. Could they afford to have the question of Trystan's murderer still open by that time? Because even if the Taavi weren't the most likely suspects, they were still the Taavi, and *if* the bastards killed Trystan only to plant Emeric on that throne...

Wouldn't that influence the dukes' decision at least a little?

'Jaghar?'

He looked up. Madelena was waiting for him, her eyebrows raised, her pen paused above the parchment.

'Yes,' he said absently. 'See what you get done at the Temple. Ask that sister's friend a couple of questions, too. If nothing comes out of it, I might as well go have a word with Hamond myself in a few days – but let's see how the investigation develops first. And continue the things I've set in motion for the past hour, finish the lists of who was where at what moment, get all the witnesses you can find.'

She nodded and scribbled down a few words. 'Anything else?'

Jaghar glanced at Velvet. She was staring into nothingness with her chin on her knees. The last minutes of the conversation seemed to have slid past her entirely.

'Can you get a few extra people to keep an eye on the princess, too? If it's Donovan, he might not be done yet.'

'Of course. Do you need them immediately?'

He hesitated for a moment. Yes, he should say, and then he ought to bring her to her room, leave for the eyes of her guardians, and return through the secret corridors minutes later...

But he didn't want to leave her alone for a single heartbeat, let alone for minutes. Demon be damned, did it matter? He wasn't going to convince Madelena of his honourable intentions anyway, and she wouldn't go around spreading the secret.

'Tomorrow morning is early enough,' he said, averting his eyes. 'I'll stay with her for tonight.'

CHAPTER 3

The network of secret corridors passed by in a haze. By the time they reached her bedroom Viviette couldn't have said how they had managed to find it, or what doors they had passed on the way to her family's tower. The world blended into a fog around her, from which only shreds of sensible thoughts loomed up to haunt her –

Father.

Dead.

The Council. The silk cloak. Emeric. And once again her father –

A knife in the back. She hadn't seen his body, thank the gods she hadn't, and yet the image hung before her as if she had witnessed the murder itself – his smiling green eyes of that afternoon, the comforting warmth of his hug, and then the blade slashing through everything she'd ever held dear about him...

'Velvet.'

Suddenly Jaghar's hands were at her shoulders, holding her painfully tightly. She looked up. Even his face swam before her eyes, crumbling together with the rest of the world – dead, her thoughts kept repeating, Father, dead, knife, back, dead. Council. Emeric. Father. Dead.

'Velvet.'

His arms lay around her the next moment, installing her on the edge of her bed between the furs and blankets. He knelt at her feet, untied her shoelaces, pulled her shoes off her feet like she was a glass doll about to break, and came up to sit beside her. Viviette closed her eyes. The soft, soothing touches of his fingers against her cold skin broke through the fog in the gentlest way possible, sparks of light in the swimming sea of nothingness that her mind had become. His fingers in her hair, tenderly taking out her braids. The soft strokes of his hands over her back as he loosened her dress and stripped it off her. His strong arms lifting her to tuck her in. Only when he had pulled the blankets over her and stepped back did she manage to look up again. Father, her thoughts still whispered, knife, dead. Jaghar was making a round through her room to check the lock on the door, the windows, the closed door behind the tapestry.

'Do you really think...'

'I have no idea what to think,' he said. His voice sounded too stiff, his strangers' voice. 'But I'm not taking risks.'

Viviette swallowed and waited, curled up underneath the blankets, until he finished his inspection and sank down on the edge of her bed again, a sharp silhouette against the glow of the coals in her hearth. For a moment the world seemed motionless, frozen. Outside this room everything had changed, turned upside down and inside out within mere hours. But here, between these four safe walls, the fire was still burning and her bed was still warm and Jaghar was still with her...

With tensed shoulders. With clenched fists. With grim shadows dancing in the depth of his eyes.

She sat up and reached for him. When her fingertips touched his shoulders, he jerked around with nearly violent shock, then sagged in her blankets and averted his face with a muffled curse. That, for the first time, silenced the persistent buzz of her thoughts.

'Jaghar?'

'I'm sorry,' he muttered. 'I'm sorry, I shouldn't...'

He didn't finish his sentence. Shouldn't what – feel things, grieve? The fog in her mind shrunk back as her concern broke through the numbness – why was he tucking *her* into bed if he was on the verge of collapsing himself?

'Jaghar...'

He remained silent, turned away from her. Viviette flicked her blankets aside and leaned over to grab his upper arm.

'Come to bed, Spymaster.'

He sighed, unbuttoned his shirt, kicked off his boots and slumped into the pillows with his trousers still on. She pulled the blankets over them and curled up against his scarred chest, hiding in his strong arms, drowning herself in the warmth of his body.

The flood of tears washed over her without a warning, a sensation of gaping emptiness in its wake – an absence so big it was almost tangible even in the unreal, incomprehensible freshness of the wound. Her father. Her *father*. Who had always been there, gentle and patient, in the background of her world, teaching her to walk, teaching her to read, teaching her to navigate through the mountains of her home – whose letters had arrived for her in Copper Coast every single week without exception –

She sobbed like a little girl against Jaghar's chest, bawling and blubbering until even the tears ran out and she was left hollow, exhausted and empty in the clammy warmth of their blankets. His strong arms didn't tremble. His breath didn't falter. But when she looked up eventually and tried to meet his gaze, he looked lost like a man waking from a nightmare.

'What are we going to *do*?' she whispered.

He closed his eyes and pulled her against him. 'You don't have to think about that now, Velvet.'

'But I *do*.' Her voice cracked as the weight of the world crashed down on her at once – the questions, the obligations, the practical arrangements. 'The Council is coming together so soon, I don't have time to waste a day crying – and you can't take it all upon yourself, this investigation, you shouldn't...'

'Velvet, please – it's my job to—'

'You're grieving too! I can't—'

'Don't say that – *I* didn't lose a father, for hell's sake!'

She pulled back from his arms, pressing her lips. The crack in his voice. The strange, lost shadows in his eyes.

'Didn't you?'

He froze. Viviette sank back into the pillows and buried her face into his chest again. His heart was pounding against his ribcage.

'Velvet...'

'I'm just trying to say,' she managed, 'that you don't need to watch over me more than I need to watch over you. There's no such thing as your job now. It's our job. I'm not going to hide here and let you deal with everything.'

He stayed silent for a good few minutes. When he eventually lifted his hand to slowly comb his fingers through her hair, he *was* trembling.

'We need to figure out who did this,' he said quietly. 'We need to figure out how we're going to keep Emeric off the throne.' His fingers tensed up. 'In two days, preferably.'

'Two days.'

'Yes.'

43

'And if we somehow manage to do all that in two days...' She took a deep breath. 'Then – they'll make me – queen of the Peaks.'

'I bloody well hope they will.'

Viviette closed her eyes. Queen. Of the Peaks. How could it feel so impossible, this destination she'd known for all her life? She had never been going anywhere else. She had never *wanted* to go anywhere else. And yet the title felt like a poorly fitting shoe to her now, an uncomfortable mistake – she had expected to be a queen *later*, when she was older and prepared for the role. Not *now*. Not as long as she was no more than some silly princess with more education on flowers than on armies. Not...

Not as long as she was still just *her*.

'But I – I might not make a good queen at all.'

Jaghar turned on his back, his arms still around her, so that she ended up lying on his chest. 'I've heard you say more sensible things, Velvet.'

'I'm serious!' Again her voice broke. 'Nobody ever prepared me to be a queen *now*! I can tell you all about decorating a dinner hall and embroidering your name in pretty calligraphy, but I have no idea how I'm going to – to manage taxes or direct an army or oversee international treaties, and...'

'And of course you'll have to figure out all of that on your own?' he suggested, with a sad smile that made her heart crumble in her chest even further.

'Well – no – but...'

'Velvet.' He came up on his elbows, forcing her to look up as well. 'Your father never got the hang of tax policies either, don't you remember? He told Sophronia what he wanted to get done, then she started calculating, came up with a plan and told your father to execute it. Every year again. Also, luckily, she's still very much alive.'

Father. The tears stung behind her eyes again at the vividness of the memories surging up in her at once – his puzzled frowns at his treasurer's reports, his muffled curses as he grew more and more frustrated over his calculations... Oh, gods. *Father*. How in the world would she learn this without his gentle instructions, his nudges in the right direction? How would she handle the prospect of never hearing his voice again?

'And there's no rush, Velvet.' Jaghar sat up and pulled her closer in his lap, resting his forehead against hers. His words were like a warm bath, pulling her in, shielding her from the cruel truths of the world outside. 'I'm still here. Your father's advisors are still here. The treaties don't need urgent changes, and the Empress would be a fool to attack us with the top of our army still in place. You don't need to be fully informed within a week.'

'Yes, but what if I never—'

'If you never learn it?' He ran his fingers through her hair. 'There's never been a single thing you haven't been able to learn. You'll be a brilliant queen. I've known you'd be since the first day I saw you for who you were.'

Viviette closed her eyes. Just a job, she'd told herself at the Floating Castle – another role she could play, as much an act as the girl behind her mask or the giggling princess. She had known how to do it by Donovan's side, before she realised who he truly was. But at least the Riverlands were his responsibility more than hers, at least she could have learned from him in the first years of her marriage.

Then again – Jaghar was right. She wasn't alone here.

'You'll stay with me, won't you? Whatever happens?'

'Velvet...' The joyless smile on his lips nearly made her burst out in tears again. 'I'll never not be on your side. I promise.'

She opened her mouth, didn't find the words, closed it again. In the faint glow of the hearth his eyes shone like black stars. There was not a trace of ingenuity on his sharp face, not even a tad of exaggeration –

Never not on her side.

Said the man whose name was spoken only on a whisper in many a foreign court, just in case he was listening along from the walls of the castles and palaces. *A good man, Vivi. A dangerous man – but a good man.*

The tears were flowing again before she could stop them. Thank you, she wanted to say. I don't know what I did to deserve this, what I did to deserve you – I don't know what I'd ever do without you. But her body spoke before her mind could. Without pausing or thinking she leaned forward and brushed her lips over his, a plea for a reassurance neither of them would ever be able to put into words, a kiss seeking the comfort of a single thing unchanged. Jaghar answered without hesitation, his breath faltering as their lips met and parted again, his eyes closed when she pulled back. But his hands remained motionless in her blankets, clenched to fists as if to strangle something.

'Sorry,' she whispered. 'If you don't want me to—'

'No.' His voice sounded choked. 'That's not what – I want you more than anything in the world, but...' He swallowed. 'It's not a healthy kind of desire now, Velvet. I'm feeling – too much of the wrong things. I'm not going to be gentle if I lose control now, and I don't want...'

He didn't finish his sentence. His body tensed up like a volcano about to erupt, every muscle and tendon tight like a bow string as the emotions he had tried to suppress came rising to the surface. Viviette swallowed. She shouldn't want this, not tonight – but the gaping void in her heart wanted nothing more than to be consumed by some feeling, *any* feeling –

'You don't need to control yourself for me.'

'Velvet...'

She pulled him closer and stopped his words with her lips. Under her hands she felt his composure break as he grabbed her around the waist and claimed her with a kiss of frantic intensity – all his love and grief and rage bundled into a single explosion of passion, capturing her, conquering her, silencing the persistent droning of her thoughts as her body surrendered to the ferocity of his embrace. Hands clawing into sides and shoulders, mouths melting together – they clung to each other in desperate, feverish closeness until she could no longer say where her body ended and his began, until she was nothing but rhythm and instinct, unable to feel even pain in the overwhelming flood of their shared agony. She barely noticed her own hands yanking open his buttons, barely noticed him jerking down his trousers. Then he was in her, thrusting deep with raw, savage need, pinning her to the mattress and fucking her as if she were the object of all his pain and fury herself...

He came with a tormented groan, spilling his hot seed as he collapsed on top of her and clawed his fingers into her sides until the most violent waves of his release died away. Panting and moaning they lay in the pillows, entangled and exhausted. With her arms around him, her face buried into the hollow of his neck, Viviette needed a moment to realise that the shudders still running through him were not the aftermath of his climax –

He was *crying*.

Curled up against her, clutching her with trembling hands, he lay sobbing in her arms – some open wound within him laid bare by his burst of passion, revealing him to the world in all his sudden vulnerability. He cried without a sound, even now, but he didn't avert his face when she bent over to kiss him softly on his forehead and clenched her arms even tighter around him.

Something hardened within her as she lay there and held him, stroking his silver hair and kissing his feverish skin until the sobbing subsided. No going back now. No giving up the fight. It didn't matter she had no idea how she could ever win the Council to her side in mere days, or how she was supposed to solve a murder she never wanted to think about again. For Jaghar's sake she'd have to figure it out. For her father's sake –

He had trusted her.

He had wanted her to do this.

She repeated the words to herself while she lay there in the deepening dark of her dying fire and held Jaghar in her arms – she wouldn't give up. She wouldn't back down. She would get what was hers and do what she had to do.

She would be a queen her father would have been proud to see.

Her mind was clear when Jaghar eventually lifted his head to answer her kisses. The panic had dissolved, the fear waned. The hollow pain still ached in her chest, but it no longer held her paralysed now – this was not the moment. She could grieve later, when all was said and done. First she had to survive, win the race for the throne, find her father's murderer. She wouldn't be weak. She wouldn't be that little girl others had to worry about. She would hold her shoulders straight and be a force to be reckoned with.

'Princess...'

'It's alright,' she whispered. 'It'll be alright. Stay with me. I don't want to let go of you tonight.'

He pulled her back against his chest, wrapping the blankets around them with trembling arms. 'But tomorrow...'

'Tomorrow,' Viviette said, nestling herself against him and closing her eyes, 'we fight.'

CHAPTER 4

Jaghar woke up with Velvet in his arms, their bodies entangled in the clammy heat of woollen blankets and furs.

In her bedroom in Rock Hall.

He had never stayed the night in her bedroom in Rock Hall.

And at that thought the memories of the past night returned to him with a sharpness that tore his heart from his chest all over again – Trystan. The knife. The dead silence of a castle in mourning and Velvet's empty eyes. He sank back into the blankets, squeezing his eyes shut – if only he could go back to sleep, forget about the world for a few more minutes...

'Jaghar?' Velvet muttered, half-asleep in his arms. He nearly cursed out loud. At the very damn least he shouldn't have woken her.

'I'm here.'

'You...'

She was quiet for a few heartbeats, tensing in his arms. Then, her voice so small he barely heard her, she said, 'It wasn't – just a nightmare.'

'I'm sorry, Velvet – I'm so...'

With a muffled sob she clenched her arms around him and buried her face against his chest. He held her, his thoughts wavering between a bottomless pit of panic and the list of tasks waiting for him – he had to find Madelena for a report of last night. Trystan was dead. The Council dukes would start arriving soon. Trystan was never coming back. Did he have the manpower to simply interrogate every foreign guest this morning? Trystan had died without his guards around. If he hadn't loitered around in that cursed garden so long yesterday, none of this may have happened in the first place...

'I'm so sorry,' he whispered again.

She lay frozen for minutes, nothing but the faint whiffs of breath over his chest to prove she was still alive and awake. Then, abruptly, she pulled from his arms and sat up, averting her face so he couldn't see the look in her eyes behind her tangled black curls.

'We have to get to work.'

Her voice sounded too hard all of a sudden, barely like her own voice. Even her movements seemed like some stranger's movements as she stepped out of bed without looking back at him – too stiff, too heavy, none of her usual light-footed elegance. She pulled a dress from her closet with so much force that two others tumbled out after it – black silk, Jaghar registered, a sting burning through his heart.

'Velvet...'

'We have two days,' she said, still not looking at him as she untangled the ribbons of her bodice with quick, practised hands. 'No time to do nothing. I have to talk with Reginald, at least, and...'

'Velvet.'

'And we have to figure out what all the dukes on the Council are planning to do. How we're going to keep them from voting for Emeric. I have to...'

'Velvet,' Jaghar repeated, flinging his blanket aside. 'Come here.'

Finally she turned towards him, the bundle of silk clutched in her bare arms. For a moment her face remained frozen in that cold, uncaring expression; then her shoulders sagged, her eyes softened. With a quiet, muffled sound she stepped back to the bed and sank down next to him on the edge of the mattress, resting her forehead against his shoulder. Her breath came a little too fast.

'That's better,' he said, running his fingers through her messy curls. 'Take a deep breath, Princess. Five minutes in the morning aren't going to make the difference. And let me get your brush.'

She nodded, her eyes closed. He stood, shot into his trousers, and grabbed his shirt from the floor and her hairbrush from the dressing table. As he sank down beside her again, he added, 'I could also talk with Reginald, in case you'd rather not...'

'You can't do everything,' she muttered.

Another sting through his heart. So it turned out, he nearly said – Trystan was dead, and Trystan wouldn't have died if he had just been in the right place at the right moment... But he pressed that thought away. Not the moment to wallow in self-doubt. *Now* at least he had to keep his head clear.

'Reginald isn't the most daunting task on my list,' he said, carefully gathering her curls on her back as he spoke. She shivered each time his fingers brushed over her shoulders. 'I'm more worried about the dukes, and about...' He hesitated. 'Whoever the murderer is.'

Velvet stiffened only for a fraction of a moment. 'Yes.'

He stayed silent as he quietly separated her hair into thinner strands, then began to untangle them, with gentle, meticulous strokes. The silk of her dark locks was soothingly familiar between his fingers, as was the softness of her neck and shoulders under his fingertips. Like all those mornings on the road – all those mornings when it had seemed the world would never turn dark again.

Only after minutes did she say, 'Can I help with the – the murder case?'

His heart twisted. 'Depends on what Madelena found during the night. I'll let you know.'

54

She nodded, then flinched as that movement caught the teeth of the brush in a nasty knot. 'And the Council?'

'Depends on the duke or duchess,' he said wryly. 'Some of them will be happy enough to vote against Emeric – at least I think Laudine might...'

A mirthless snigger escaped her before he could finish his sentence. 'What did she call him again? A small man with a big opinion of himself?'

'In all fairness,' Jaghar said, unable to suppress half a smile at the memory of that midwinter ball six years ago, 'he accused her of cuckolding her late husband. I think she was quite polite for the circumstances.'

'Oh, that was the reason? Father wouldn't tell me.' She hesitated for a moment longer, then added, 'I think Wymond might also consider voting for me if he hears of Father's plans.'

'I damn well hope so.' The duke had been one of Trystan's closest personal friends – and if Jaghar recalled correctly, he had spoken about Emeric with obvious dislike at more than one recent occasion. 'So that could be two of them.'

'And the rest?'

The question left an unpleasantly wary silence behind. Jaghar finished untangling the last few knots, then sighed and said, 'I'm not sure about the rest.'

She turned towards him, curls tumbling over her bare shoulders. 'Gideon is going to vote for Emeric, I suppose.'

'Gideon is a cocky, mud-brained coward,' Jaghar muttered, and a feeble smile broke through on her face.

'Is that your professional opinion, Spymaster?'

'My personal opinion is significantly less polite,' he said, unable to suppress a sour grin. 'Gideon is a lost case, if you ask me. Too amiable with Emeric, too proud to ever change his mind. But the others...'

He fell silent, considering the rest of them. Osric the diamond smuggler would likely vote for whoever would keep him safe from the gallows – assuming he had nothing to do with Trystan's death in the first place. Aldred, law-abiding to a fault, would choose the candidate the official guidelines preferred, which was technically still Emeric at the moment. The last two, Gerald and Eluard... He didn't know the two men all that well. It seemed unwisely optimistic to assume both of them would support the candidature of a young girl they barely knew, let alone knew in her full capacity.

Velvet frowned before he even opened his mouth. 'The others might be just as problematic as Gideon.'

'Might be,' he admitted, biting his frustration away. 'Still – we should be able to come up with *something*.'

'Threatening to reveal their shameful secrets to the world if they vote for Emeric?' she said wryly. 'But that won't make them easier to handle afterwards.'

'No. Although I suppose Gideon would go to serious lengths to hide those three extramarital children he's secretly providing for, but...'

Her eyes widened. 'Oh, *really*.'

'Certainly,' Jaghar said, grimacing. 'Two different mistresses, pretty ugly business. But you're right – he's going to be unpleasant for the rest of his life if we force him to vote against his dear old friend that way. Or he might run to Emeric to tell him what's going on as soon as we take our eyes off him. Wouldn't help either.'

'No.' She muttered a curse. 'We could try to close a deal with Osric, I suppose? The problem is...'

'A vote for you in exchange for a quick acquittal on the diamond issue?'

'Exactly. But then we'd have a duke with Taavi sympathies at our border.'

Jaghar sighed. 'Yes, and he knows Emeric would probably let it go too, so he might still just as well vote for him. I could...'

Knuckles at the door interrupted him, followed by a maid's hesitant voice. 'Your Highness? Your Highness, are you here?'

'Oh, hell's sake,' Velvet muttered, stiffening up. Then, louder, 'What is it, Nora?'

'Lord Gideon is arriving at Rock Hall in a few minutes, Your Highness. Would you like me to help you prepare?'

'A moment!'

'You don't have to go,' Jaghar said, even though she had already jumped up, grabbing for hair ribbons and underdresses. 'There's really not much to lose with the bastard, he won't suddenly vote for you just because you're there to welcome him. If you'd rather stay out of sight a little longer...'

'The rest of the court will notice if I'm not there.' She glanced at the door, then at him, her eyes gleaming a little too brightly. 'Even if I don't care about *his* opinion...'

He closed his eyes. 'Yes. You're right.'

'Will I see you?'

'As soon as I've spoken with Madelena. Or join us, if you have the time.'

A smile – a miniscule, but grateful smile – slid over her face. With leaden limbs and a foggy mind Jaghar stood up, pulled her closer and pressed a kiss to her forehead. It took a little too much effort to let go of her again. He had let Trystan out of sight for five minutes too long already. Not a mistake he could make a second time. Not a mistake *he* would survive a second time.

'Your Highness?' the maid repeated outside, and he steeled himself and stepped back.

'Be careful, Velvet.'

'You too,' she whispered. 'I'll see you as soon as possible.'

Jaghar watched Lord Gideon arrive from a shadowy corner of the courtyard, hidden from the watching eyes of the court. The duke of the Wild Vales arrived accompanied by a crowd of servants, knights, his wife and his sons, and two full coaches of luggage. In some mysterious way, the family appeared to have packed half their household in the few hours between the news of Trystan's death and their departure from home; servant girls ran around with gowns that had to cost twice an average dowry.

Gowns for a coronation. His heart shrivelled to a painful lump of lead in his chest. Trystan would have shaken his head and gently remarked that it was quite strange how people felt the urge to celebrate a knife landing into a king's back with so much splendour...

Even in the crawling chaos of the noble arrivals, he noticed Velvet the moment she stepped out onto the courtyard in her black gown, the unwavering smile plastered upon her face looking like a cry for help. Behind her came Emeric, whose black costume seemed a matter of obligation – at least the king's brother greeted Gideon with broad grins and elated gestures that would better fit a summer solstice ball than a funeral. Gideon barely stopped to acknowledge Velvet's existence at all. Only his wife stood still to curtsy and tie on a quick, unsmiling conversation while the men already ambled inside.

A little too late did Jaghar realise his hand was resting on the hilt of his knife. The bastards, the bloody bastards... His limbs were itching to move, to shove every idiot around her out of the way, take her in his arms and kiss the pain out of her in the plain light of day if he had to – but the world was still looking, and how would she explain his madness to the Council?

So he stayed where he stood, clenching his teeth until his jaws hurt, his eyes glued to the shadows on Velvet's face. Finally she turned away and disappeared back inside. Only then did he tear his hand away from the weapon at his belt and release the breath locked in his lungs. Demon be damned, if only this bloody secrecy hadn't been so necessary. If only...

'Jaghar?'

He jolted around. Paulette had appeared behind him, her face even paler than usual. Not much sleep for the past night, he assumed.

'What is it?'

'Madelena sent me to give you a quick update. About Osric.'

'Oh, yes – you had him tonight?' He closed his eyes for a fraction of a heartbeat. Damn the fury, the exhaustion, his heart twisting in his chest with every other thought of Trystan – he had to focus on his job now. If for no other reason, Velvet needed him to. 'Anything interesting?'

Paulette grimaced. 'He's been celebrating the entire night – kept saying that Emeric would never cause so much trouble about his unseemly diamond businesses with the Taavi. Then again, he seemed genuinely surprised by the state of affairs. So I think you can keep him on your list of bastards who need some more juridical trouble after them, but as a murderer I don't give him much chance.'

Jaghar averted his gaze, suppressing a curse. More or less celebrating. The entire night. For the death of a man who had done more for the world every single day than bloody Osric ever contributed to anything in his life. Some more juridical trouble was the least of measures he'd want to take...

But not a murderer. A case for later, then.

'Thanks,' he said, too curt. 'And he assumes it's going to be Emeric?'

Paulette frowned. 'Well – yes? Don't you assume so? The princess isn't married, the laws are pretty clear.'

'Trystan planned to have her married by now.'

'Yes, but she ran away.'

Jaghar again suppressed the urge to curse. From a marriage from hell, yes. Back to a father who wanted her on his throne. If only Trystan had survived a single day more ... For the twentieth time that morning he found himself wondering whether the timing wasn't a little *too* bad – but then again, who in the world could have spread the news of the king's decision?

'Never mind,' he said flatly. 'We'll see. Could you take a look around Gideon for the rest of the day?'

Paulette gave him a messy salute and hurried off again. He should have given her time to sleep, he realised just too late. On the other hand, they could all sleep again by the time the Council meeting was behind them, and if anyone truly burnt out, Madelena wouldn't hesitate to intervene.

Until then...

He had a murder to solve. And what in the world was he going to do with the Council?

He strode back into the castle, found Madelena buried in notes in the office, and learned that nobody of interest had been seen around Trystan's study at the right time, although some people had been rather vague about their movements. He left some instructions about which foreign diplomats to interrogate or shadow in more subtle ways, noted down a quick list of people he needed a word with himself, and gave permission for the king's body to be moved as long as the rest of the room was left untouched. There was no doubt about the cause of death anyway, and in the very least Velvet should be able to see her father in slightly less shocking circumstances somewhere today.

Then he wandered through the shadows of the castle, trying to think about the murder he was supposed to solve, and brooding only about the Council instead. Two more nights, then the dukes of the Peaks would come together to vote. Two more nights, and he'd know whether his ill-timed absence had cost Velvet the throne of her kingdom.

Emeric, Osric assumed. That was one vote for Trystan's brother. Gideon had been unsubtle as expected, too – so that made two out of seven Council votes already. Of the three remaining votes, at least two would have to go to Velvet, and he didn't dare to be hopeful about bloody Aldred with his bloody laws...

Jaghar sank down in the windowsill of a deserted corridor and suppressed a groan. What to do?

The forceful way wouldn't do. Of course, there would be guilty secrets. He could find them, too. But Velvet was right, it wouldn't help if she had to start her reign amidst several deeply disgruntled dukes. The world was troublesome enough without some of the most important men in her kingdom opposing her from the very first day.

Somehow he'd have to convince them. Somehow he'd have to make them see how utterly brilliant and capable and qualified she was – or if he couldn't manage that much within mere days, at the very least he'd have to show them that Emeric was a worse alternative. Old friendships with the Taavi. No interest in ruling a kingdom whatsoever. As unmarried as Velvet, despite being close to twice her age – who would ever consider him a reasonable option at all?

He closed his eyes, his fingers reaching for his knife again. A bunch of old idiots. The kind of men who saw nothing but a marriageable asset in any woman of noble birth. The kind that...

'Spymaster?'

He jolted around. A lanky servant stood at a safe distance of several arm lengths, his eyes a tad too wide. Only then did it occur to Jaghar that perhaps he should stop clutching his knife like a man about to commit a murder.

'What?'

'Prince Emeric asks for you, Spymaster. As soon as possible, he said.'

Jaghar only barely swallowed a curse. 'Any specific reason?'

'I don't know, Spymaster.' The young man's nose trembled. Perhaps he shouldn't have snapped so brusquely either. 'He – he said it was urgent. I'm sorry, I don't know—'

'Never mind,' Jaghar interrupted, steeling himself. 'I'll go see him.'

Emeric did vaguely resemble his older brother, at least in the details – the same bright green eyes, the same dark curls, the same strong, straight nose. But his smile was cocky rather than friendly, and his puffy cheeks gave him an air of chronic pomposity. Like a bloated goat, Velvet had once whispered during dinner. Even now, with the weight of Trystan's absence burdening every footstep, Jaghar nearly chuckled at the memory.

'You asked for me?'

Your Highness, he should have said according to the rules of this land. Prince, he should at least have added in accordance with his Androughan habits. But his stomach revolted at the sight of Emeric's satisfied near-grin, and pressing an honorific title over his lips was more than he could persuade himself to do.

The other man clearly noticed the omission. At least the contentment in his expression melted away for a heartbeat.

'Ah, Jaghar. Yes. Take a seat.'

Jaghar sat down in the visitor's chair at the prince's desk – half a foot lower than Emeric's own chair. A ridiculously transparent attempt to make him feel intimidated. It only added another spark of anger to the fire already roaring through his chest.

He waited. Judging by the frown on Emeric's face, the thin silence conveyed his opinions well enough.

'Well,' the prince eventually said, folding his hands as he leaned back in his chair. 'I suppose you understand why I wanted to see you. You've been investigating my brother's death already, I assume? I'd like to hear about your progress so far.'

He looked far too pleased with himself. Was he *enjoying* the situation? In the past years the man had never shown any interest in actual politics, strategies, or negotiations – so little that Jaghar simply assumed he had no desire to be king at all. And yet there was no trace of nervousness on Emeric now, no reluctance, none of the doubts and fears that had held even Velvet in their terrifying grip over the past night. What did the bastard think – that looking down on others and commanding them around was all it took to rule a kingdom?

Somehow Jaghar managed not to scoff.

'I'm afraid I can't tell you about the investigation yet,' he said, holding the prince's gaze. 'It's ongoing, indeed. That's all I'm allowed to say.'

Emeric uttered an incredulous laugh. 'All you're allowed to say? Who in the world is forbidding you to tell *me* about—'

'Technically speaking, *Prince*,' Jaghar interrupted, with a little too much emphasis on that last word, 'the Peaks don't have a king or queen until the Council has cast its votes, and the death of a king is a classified matter I'm allowed to discuss only with the legal ruler of the kingdom. I can tell you about my findings only if, and after, the Council appoints you.'

He wasn't sure if the juridical details were entirely correct, but he *was* sure Emeric didn't know his law books any better than he did, and at least it sounded like a more acceptable argument than simply the fact that he'd rather die than help the windbag.

Emeric's face reddened. 'You have to admit that this is a rather ridiculous reason not to inform me about my own brother's death.'

'I didn't write the law books,' Jaghar said, with a shrug. 'Anything else I can do for you? If not, I'd prefer to continue working on—'

'Now wait a moment,' Emeric snapped. 'I wasn't done yet, Spymaster. You can't simply keep this investigation hidden from the royal family – I know Trystan barely bothered to keep an eye on you, but you cannot honestly believe we'll leave this matter unsupervised?'

'We don't. I'm supervising it.'

'What – you think you can play king of the Peaks for two days?'

'I'm playing Spymaster, Prince,' Jaghar said coldly. 'As I've quite successfully done for the past eight years.'

'And you believe you can decide—'

'I didn't decide anything. The laws did.' He leaned forward, and quite to his satisfaction Emeric shrunk back an inch.

'You can't want me to wait—'

'If you believe the Council will indeed appoint you, you'll hear all details of my investigation in two days. I see no reason to violate the law for such a short time.'

'And what if the killer comes after me as well?' Emeric snapped. 'I should be aware of any threats to my life, don't you think?'

'Ah,' Jaghar said, and smiled. He shouldn't, he really shouldn't, but the memory of Trystan's gentle tact burnt in him with sickening grief, and this pompous, aggressive idiot brought it to the surface in all the wrong ways. 'You're scared, I understand?'

Emeric hesitated a moment too long, his lips already apart. 'Well – no – of course I'm not...'

His objection died away without a conclusion. Jaghar waited. The prince again cleared his throat and continued, 'It's a matter of the wellbeing of this kingdom. We can't lose *two* royals within a week.'

'Ah. The wellbeing of the kingdom.' Coming from a man who had always prioritised his dinner to any urgent military meeting. 'Well, allow me to reassure you – of course I'll let you know if you appear to be in danger, but so far it seems highly unlikely that the person who killed Trystan will target you as well. Does that—'

'What's *that* supposed to mean?'

Jaghar raised an eyebrow, hiding his surprise only with effort. Not scared, Emeric had hastened to clarify, and yet that snapped question came out with an obvious undercurrent of alarm.

'Does that upset you?'

'Are you saying...' Emeric leaned over the table, with another mirthless chuckle. 'Are you saying someone killed my brother for *personal* reasons?'

Personal – what was personal? In all likeliness, Trystan had been killed for being a decent man with integrity – too lawful to let even a powerful duke get away with smuggling, too principled to allow a High Priest to fondle his Temple girls, too much a loving father to send his daughter back into the hands of a monster... None of those main suspects had much to fear from Emeric. Even Donovan would probably rather see Trystan's brother on the throne than Velvet herself.

'A possibility,' he said, getting to his feet. 'Now if you don't mind – work is calling. If you have any questions I can legally answer, let me know.'

Emeric didn't reply as Jaghar turned around and made for the door – too stupefied to object, it seemed. Only when Jaghar reached for the door handle did the prince snap, 'This is not how I expect you to treat me in the future, Spymaster.'

Jaghar turned around, his reflexes fighting his attempts to stay calm. 'Beg your pardon?'

'Perhaps Trystan didn't mind you wandering around as if you owned the castle, but I won't allow this kind of nonsense, do you understand that? I expect respect and obedience from my people, and if you're unable to behave appropriately...' A scornful snort. 'I'll be more than happy to find myself a Spymaster who doesn't feel so inclined to act like some Androughan savage. Did I make myself clear?'

Jaghar didn't move. Moving, he was painfully aware, would probably send his fists straight into Emeric's puffy, pompous face. For Velvet's sake, he couldn't afford to be thrown out of Rock Hall before sunset.

'You are clearer than you know you are, Prince,' he said, and turned to leave.

CHAPTER 5

The bastard – the bloody *bastard.*

Viviette barely refrained from smashing a few candlesticks into the walls as she hurried through the castle, away from the courtyard – away from damned Gideon, with his insufferable arrogant grin. Away from Emeric, too, basking in the sunlight like he had already been crowned, like he hadn't lost a brother mere hours ago. Tears stung mercilessly behind her eyes. She couldn't burst out crying in the middle of a crowd – she wouldn't be weak, wouldn't be a trouble to others – but *Father...*

She reached the deserted garden, eventually, and stumbled outside with nobody but two of Jaghar's men following behind her. Half-hidden from view by two large rhododendrons, she sank down on the low stone edges of a plant trough and buried her face in her hands, sucking in deep, shivering breaths to bring her heartbeat down.

Father.

Father.

What was she doing here, trying to act like some regal puppet while she only wanted to curl up in bed and cry until sunset? Bloody Gideon didn't care whether she was there to receive him – *none* of them cared. For all she knew, Reginald would laugh her out of his office if she told him she wanted to keep Emeric off the throne, and then what was she going to do? What if nobody...

I'll never not be on your side, Velvet.

Jaghar.

And then she cried anyway, the tears leaking from her eyes despite her best attempts to stop them. *Jaghar.* Who had clutched to her through the night as though she were his last chance at life, muttered her name in his dreams on a harrowed, broken whisper that sent shivers through her at the memory alone. He wouldn't laugh at her, not to save his life – but then again, he might still wreck himself in his attempts to save *her* life, and then what would she do?

I could talk with Reginald. As if he didn't have enough on his mind yet. As if his heart wasn't cracking in his chest at the thought of that damned investigation alone. More than anything she wanted to go find him and hide in his arms until all of this was over, whatever the end would be – but she *couldn't*. She wasn't going to be weak. She wasn't going to cause him any more worries. She would do what she had to do and save herself for once.

But it took her minutes to get the flow of tears under control, and even when it had long dried up, she couldn't get her feet to move and carry her back into the castle. Going back meant facing the world again. Facing a Rock Hall without her father again. Facing people who could destroy her last hopes and dreams with a few simple refusals, facing...

'Viviette?' a familiar voice said behind her.

She jerked around. A tall man with silver sideburns and a long, narrow face had shown up in the empty garden behind her, dressed in a black travelling cloak and leather riding boots. She so little expected to see him that it took her a moment to recognise him –

'Wymond?'

'Glad to hear I haven't grown unrecognizably old yet,' the duke said, with a joyless smile. 'I'd rather have seen you again under other circumstances, but...'

'You're so early! Good gods, did you ride for the entire night?'

'I wouldn't have slept anyway after the pigeon with Emeric's letter arrived. At the very least I had to know...' He stepped forward and laid his hands on her shoulders, like he had done when she was still a little girl proud to demonstrate her knowledge of multiplication tables. His voice sank to a low, concerned tone. 'Are *you* safe? Is someone keeping an eye on you?

For all we know that damned murderer is still walking around, and...'

'Please don't worry too much,' Viviette said, managing something that came reasonably close to a confident smile, even if it was joyless as the grave. 'If you look over your shoulder you'll see a few of Jaghar's men at the door – they're not leaving me out of sight until he has found the murderer. I'll be safe.'

Underneath the coarse wool of his mantle, Wymond's shoulders relaxed a little. 'Thank the gods for Jaghar, once again. What we'd do without him...'

Viviette nodded, averting her face. Wymond's hands on her shoulders tensed up even tighter.

'Vivi – no, Viviette, I should probably say. You're not twelve anymore.'

She laughed despite herself, although it came out sounding rather like a sob. 'You can call me Vivi until my dying day – I'd say you deserve at least that much for riding me around on your back for hours.'

Despite the bags under his eyes and the lines on his face, his laugh was still as full as she had ever known it. For a minuscule moment her heart felt a little lighter.

'Very well, Vivi. Do you mind if I sit down? It's been a tiring ride.'

'Good gods, of course I don't mind – did you storm straight into the garden after you jumped off your horse?'

'More or less.' He sank down on the stone edge beside her and loosened his cloak. Squinting against the sunlight, he looked up to her and added, 'You're looking more composed than I'd dared to hope, to tell you the truth. I was afraid – after the mess with that Riverlands bag of shit – pardon me the wording – followed by a shock of this magnitude, you'd...'

'Lay crying between the magnolias?'

He managed a bitter smile. 'I couldn't have blamed you. It must have been horrible to...'

Viviette took a deep breath to soothe the nausea roaring up in her. To find him. Father. Dead. A deadly, dark emptiness was rattling at the harness on her heart – never before had she understood so well how much Jaghar needed his heartless façade to survive.

'I'm trying not to think too much about it now, Wymond. Not until – I mean, there's so much that needs to be arranged now.'

'You don't have to arrange anything if you don't—'

'He's my *father*.'

Was, her thoughts bitterly corrected her, he *was* your father – but she couldn't bring that correction over her lips. Wymond examined her for a moment longer, then averted his face, pulled a water bag from his belt, and took a generous sip. Lowering the water again, he slowly said, 'What do you want to arrange?'

Viviette hesitated, then settled herself beside him and wrapped her arms around herself. Could she tell him? Perhaps she should stay out of the Council meddling entirely and leave it to Jaghar to steer the dukes in the right direction – but Jaghar had enough to do, and if she couldn't trust her father's old friend, there was nobody she could trust.

'There's something you need to know about what happened yesterday morning. The morning before – before he died.'

He turned towards her, rubbing his long sideburns, his eyes earnest but calm.

'We spoke about the future,' Viviette said, swallowing another wave of sickness, 'whether I should enter another engagement anywhere soon. He – well, I don't need to repeat everything, but he decided I wouldn't have to. That he'd make me his heir even if I wasn't married yet. He was planning to arrange it within a few days.'

Wymond didn't even blink, but his face sank even further. 'Good gods. Do you think someone killed him because of that decision?'

'Not really – how should anyone have known about the decision in the first place? I knew and Jaghar knew, and Reginald – his secretary – but as far as I know, nobody else heard about it yet.'

'Awfully coincidental, though.'

'It is, but it *must* be.'

The duke turned back around and rubbed his face, muttering a curse. 'Even if it is a coincidence – well, the consequences are the same, I suppose.'

'You mean – Emeric is still his heir.'

'Emeric,' Wymond grumbled, 'shouldn't be the heir to a single bedroom, let alone to a kingdom. The boy has been worthless from the start and only grown worse. But I don't suppose everyone on the Council will share that opinion.'

Viviette barely dared to breathe. Seven votes. She needed four. Wymond alone wouldn't achieve much. And yet – the idea that even a single duke might actually trust her enough to cast a vote in her name, someone who wasn't Jaghar...

'You'll need witnesses,' Wymond said, shaking his head. 'Ask Reginald to make a statement during our meeting. Get every bit of evidence you can find – did Trystan write any notes about his plan? Letters? I can't guarantee it will be enough, but by the bloody gods, we can't just sit by while some murderous burglar is putting Emeric into your place.'

'You mean – you'll help me?'

'I'm offended you dared to doubt that in the first place, Vivi,' he said with a watery smile. 'I remember how you convinced Trystan to let you take riding lessons when you were barely eight years old. A kingdom will give you less trouble.'

She nearly flung her arms around him as if she were still that same impatient eight-year-old, then remembered that twelve years had passed since, that dozens of people might be watching her from the windows towering over them, and that she was trying to give the impression that she could handle a coronation in two nights. Not a weak little girl. Not a problem.

'I'm not sure how I can ever thank you enough,' she said, averting her eyes.

From the corner of her eyes she could see him examining her with a concerned expression on his long face, like their physician examining her when she came down with a flu. 'The best you can do is stay on your feet, Vivi.'

'I will.' Somehow it didn't come out as strongly as she wanted. 'Don't worry. I will.'

'Reginald?'

'Your Highness?' The young blond man at the desk jolted around, nearly dropping a pile of parchment. His face was pale as wax, his eyes a little red. 'Oh, goodness, I'm so sorry, it is an absolute mess here – I've been trying to reorganise—'

'Please, please!' she interrupted his rattling, closing the door behind her. 'I'm the one who comes falling into your office without any warning – don't worry about it. Could we have a little word? Or any other moment today, if you're...'

'No, no, please take a seat!' He waved uncomfortably at the single chair not occupied by towering piles of notes. 'I was hoping I'd see you one of these days – I didn't dare to disturb you after – after...'

He looked away and sniffed quietly; it took a few heartbeats before he turned back to her again.

'I'm sorry,' he muttered, blinking profusely. 'I'm not being myself. Please, what can I do for you, Your Highness?'

She felt strangely ashamed, for a moment, about her own cold-bloodedness. Why wasn't she forcing back tears like the poor boy was – what would he *think* of her? But if she collapsed now, she wouldn't get up again...

'I wanted to ask you about the last conversation you had with my father. You did speak with him yesterday afternoon, didn't you?'

Reginald nodded quickly, his blond curls dancing around his head. 'Yes, we did.' His voice sank to a nervous whisper. 'I suppose this is about your – your...'

'Yes.'

'Thank the gods, Your Highness, I've been fretting about it all night. Could you tell me – if I may be so free?' He swallowed audibly. 'The Spymaster woke me yesterday to ask if I told anyone about the king's decision – do you have any idea – did they kill him because – because...'

'You didn't tell anyone, did you?'

'Of course I didn't!'

'Then it really can't have been because of me,' Viviette said, closing her eyes. Was she trying to reassure herself or the young man standing before her? Wymond had said it as well, the timing was nearly *too* suspicious... 'Nobody knew except for you and me and Jaghar. It must have been – well, anything else, but the problem is...'

'That it's brought you in trouble as well? Yes, of course.'

She looked up again. He was staring at her with wide open eyes and clenched lips, like a tense lapdog waiting for an order. The little spark of hope Wymond had lit in her chest flared up to nearly a small flame.

'So – would you be willing to help me with this?'

'Of course, of course!' He looked shocked. 'The king wanted you to inherit his throne. Helping you is the very least I could do. Just tell me where you need me, who I need to tell my story, and I'll be there.'

Something like a smile broke through the detached, impassive blur of her mind. A witness. She had a *witness*, someone even the most sceptical Council members could hardly accuse of lying for his own interests.

'You have no idea how much of a relief that is, Reginald.' She jumped up, a surge of energy flowing through her for the first time that day. 'I think the most important thing is that you tell the Council about Father's plans when they meet – could you do that?'

'Yes, of course!'

'Good – and is there any other evidence? Any notes or letters? Even any allusions to his plan might already be helpful.'

'I don't think there are any letters with his exact plans, Your Highness.' He blushed. 'I'm really sorry, he really only told me to prepare some necessary articles for the change of law he'd need.'

Viviette tilted her head. His blush was too shrill a contrast to his pale face to ignore – and was it her imagination, or did he avoid her eyes now? No letters with her father's *exact* plans. Had he slipped up and hinted at the upcoming developments in any of his writing?

'Reginald, are you sure nobody else could possibly know?'

'Yes, yes, very sure!' He blushed even deeper. 'Please, Your Highness, of course I'd tell you immediately if I thought I knew anything that could help the Spymaster to solve...'

'But there's something you're not telling me, isn't there?'

He went silent, shutting his mouth as if he had swallowed something too big for his throat. His face bright red now, he averted his eyes and whispered, 'I – I wrote my aunt.'

'What?'

'My aunt – Lady Laudine.' He barely breathed the words. 'I'm so sorry, I really shouldn't have, but she's had a terrible fight with Prince Emeric a few years back, and I thought she'd enjoy knowing – well, you'll understand...'

Viviette blinked. Laudine. Reginald's aunt, she should have remembered it – and even he thought she would enjoy the thought of Emeric losing his throne? She probably shouldn't be cheering, but the small fire burning in her chest damn well felt like it.

'That – that's fine, Reginald. Your letter probably hadn't even reached her when – yesterday evening. So let's just say it's additional evidence rather than a problem, alright?'

He bowed, the relief palpable. 'Thank you so much, Your Highness – I'm sorry, I'll never—'

'Don't mention it again.' She waved his apologies away. 'It's alright, really. What else do we have?'

'Let me take a look – I'm afraid there's really not much, unless you count my copies of the current inheritance articles as evidence...'

He bent over the desk, muttering as he browsed through what looked like his youngest pile of parchment. Viviette stepped closer, examining the writing flashing by – letters, notes of past week's meetings, a schedule for the coming days that her father would never follow...

She averted her eyes, forcing back the gall from her throat. Don't think about that now, Velvet. Don't think about how he made his plans, about how he still expected to see the sunrise of this morning – don't –

Her gaze fell on the ring lying on the edge of the desk, and her stomach turned.

His ring. The golden signet ring with the small image of the eagle, her family's seal – the ring she played with when she was still young enough to sit in his lap. He must have left it in his secretary's office after their last meeting, as he did so often when he didn't want to be disturbed for every single letter that needed to be sealed. Reginald would likely have returned it this morning if the world hadn't turned upside down so cruelly in the meantime...

She looked up. The young man was still going through his pile, slower now.

Without making a sound, she stretched out her hand. Under her fingers the gold felt so cold that her heart faltered for an instant. Hell's sake, what had she expected, to still feel the warmth of his hands glowing in the metal? She quietly clenched her fist around the ring and pulled back her hand. Reginald didn't notice when she slipped it into the pocket of her coat.

'I'm sorry,' he muttered, 'I really don't think we have anything else.'

'That's alright,' Viviette said. Her heart was pounding in her chest, but her fingers refused to let go off the gold in her pocket – his ring, *his* ring, more part of him than the crown or even the silk cloak he only wore at special occasions... 'I'm more than happy if you can tell the Council what he said yesterday. That's all you need to do. Although, of course, if you happen to find anything helpful in the meantime...'

'I will let you know immediately, Your Highness,' he said hastily, bowing again. 'And please let me know if there is anything else I can do. I'll be immensely happy to help.'

And that, Viviette concluded as she stepped into the bleak corridors again, her fist still closed around her father's ring, made for a grand total of two people who didn't seem to expect she'd be a catastrophe of a queen.

'Your Highness?'

Could nobody leave her to herself for even half a minute on this day from hell? She turned around in the dark corridor, drawing her composure around herself again like one might tighten a coat. Behind her, a servant girl with red eyes was fidgeting with her hands.

'Yes?'

'Your Highness, your father is – ready. In his bedroom.'

Ready. As if he were about to leave for a trip to the valleys, packing his last books and gloves. Viviette tried to breathe in and barely managed. Suddenly she remembered again how violently Jaghar had shoved her away from the doorway last night, shielding her from the sight of that knife in his back.

Did she even want to see him?

But she was still not weak. She was still not a crying, whining mess.

'Thank you,' she managed, clenching her fist around his ring. 'I'll go see him. Could you go find the Spymaster and ask him to meet me in my rooms in an hour or so?'

'The – Spymaster?'

'Thank you.'

She felt the girl's eyes between her shoulder blades as she walked off, her knees trembling underneath the dark silk of her dress. Perhaps she should wait for Jaghar to come with her. Perhaps she shouldn't even try to face her father's dead body without his arms around her, no matter what the court would whisper.

But she remembered his blank eyes when he returned from the study last night, the sobs rocking through his body. If she asked him to come, he would – whether he could handle it or not. How could she force that confrontation upon him a second time? Hell's sake, if she wanted to rule a kingdom, this should be the least she could do on her own...

A single guard stood at the bedroom door. Guarding what, she wanted to ask – the gold on his clothes? But she didn't say a word, and he stepped aside without asking questions.

The bedroom was dusky and cold as an ice cave. No fire in the hearth, only the two candles on both sides of the bed. Between them, wrapped in the most expensive silk and goldthread...

A stranger.

She stood frozen at the foot of the bed, unable to lift her eyes of the stiff, yellowish face before her. His eyes closed, his mouth forced shut in a permanent, unnaturally serene smile. His dark beard cut short and styled with so much care that it looked like a greasy shadow under his chin. His hands folded over his chest, his nails blackening already. Nothing about him looked like the father she had known, the father who had held her in his warm arms no more than a day before – as if they had replaced his body with some wax puppet only vaguely modelled after him.

Somehow she managed to step closer, clenching her fist around the ring in her pocket and fighting her quickening breath. Her shadow fell over his face, and he still didn't move. He still didn't start breathing. He still didn't open his eyes and smile at her, that gentle smile she knew like the softness of her old baby blanket. A strange, sweet smell of rot reached her nostrils, and didn't let go again.

'Father...'

But she wasn't speaking to her father anymore, and only then did the last parts of her mind lose the hope she would ever see him again.

CHAPTER 6

Madelena's afternoon update was short, clear, and utterly unhelpful. None of the nobles from the Higher Riverlands gave the impression they had recently killed a king; none of them had been seen around Trystan's room either. If the Taavi were involved, they managed to keep very quiet on it as well. Hamond, the High Priest who couldn't keep his hands to himself, hadn't even been around the castle and stayed far away since the discovery of Trystan's body – which might be seen as a suspicious sign, Madelena admitted, but then again, the man never spent much time around Rock Hall.

And they still couldn't find any suspicious movements around Trystan's rooms. No people who had been slipping in and out of their bedroom while they were not supposed to have moved. For the evidence, the murderer might as well have climbed through the king's window and flown out again after his gruesome deed.

'Starting to sound a lot like something the Taavi could come up with,' Jaghar muttered. It didn't make much sense, he knew, suspecting anyone because of a lack of evidence. But it was hard to imagine that Hamond, who earned his money with hollow speeches and mindless chants, would have covered his traces so thoroughly, and although Donovan was admittedly capable of locking a woman in a tower for years without anyone noticing...

Would he have been able to arrange a similar operation from a distance, with barely a few weeks to prepare?

'But Trystan shouldn't have continued working with Kusti or any of his men ambling around the room,' Madelena said, biting on her pencil, and Jaghar muttered a curse.

'No.'

He forced himself to let go of his suspicions towards the Empress for a moment. Obsessing about the Taavi would only make him overlook clues – but they were such reassuring subjects exactly *because* he knew how their plans usually worked out... If the Empress was behind the murder, at least his absence from Trystan's room wouldn't be his fault. At least then he could trust they'd have kept him away from the king as long as they needed anyway, whether he had followed Velvet into that garden or not. At least then his decision of that moment hadn't made a difference between life and death...

A knock on the door. When he turned around, a black-dressed servant girl had already stuck her head into the office.

'Oh, Spymaster, there you are – thank the gods – the princess asked for you.'

He was already standing. Behind him Madelena said, 'Can we take two minutes to finish our meeting or is it urgent?'

'I – I don't think it is terribly urgent – Her Highness asked for the Spymaster to come see her in an hour, but I'm afraid it then took me about an hour to find you...'

Demon be damned. Perhaps he should try to be a little less invisible every now and then. Biting away his frustration, Jaghar curtly said, 'Tell her I'll be there in a moment.'

The girl nodded and left. When he turned back to the desk, Madelena was giving him the most sceptical look he had ever seen on her sympathetic face.

'What?' he snapped.

'Didn't think I'd live to see this day,' she said, putting her notes on the ever-growing pile. 'You could have found yourself a more accessible girl to neglect your work for, though.'

'Think I didn't notice?'

'I'm not criticising you.'

Jaghar dropped back into his chair. 'Thanks. So what is your point?'

'Just...' She sighed and tucked a blonde curl back into her messy bun. 'I don't suppose you've ever considered asking anyone to give you a hand with this mess?'

'I'm technically committing treason,' he said. The words left a sour taste in his mouth. 'Not really a situation to bring up over a glass of wine.'

'No, I suspected such a thing.'

'Why would you—'

'Jaghar.' She rarely interrupted him, and never with this look – as if he were some unwitting child rather than her employer. 'You can't spend all your time solving a murder if you're also trying to comfort a grieving princess every minute of the day. You might want to stop trying to do both nonetheless. I can take over – but it's easier if you let me know beforehand than if you try to do it yourself first and don't manage.'

He looked away, her gaze still burning in his skin. Giving work out of hand. It had never in his life been a serious option, and it should be even less when it came to finding Trystan's murderer – but he was too late to save his king anyway, and at least Velvet could still use his help.

A single day, he told himself. A few hours. Madelena was right. She had taken over for weeks – she could keep the wheels running for a single afternoon too.

'We should find out whether there's anyone else with a motive around,' he said, staring at the wall. 'Someone should have a word with the circle around Emeric – Gideon is an interesting one, and Osric might still know a couple of things even if he isn't the murderer. Alerting some of their friends to the existence of the service may help.'

She made a few quick notes. 'Will do.'

'Good. And get someone on Hamond. May at least get him nervous enough to keep his hands off those poor girls.'

Madelena sighed. 'Noted. Anything else?'

'Whatever you can think of.' He got to his feet and turned back to her. Somehow she still looked concerned rather than reproachful – did she fully realise he was leaving all the work to her to hide somewhere in a royal bedroom himself? 'And let me know if anything urgent comes up.'

'Where do I find you?'

He threw a glance over his shoulder, although he already knew the door was closed. It still felt unnatural, acknowledging this entire affair to any other living soul, even if it was the first person he'd trust after Velvet herself.

'If I'm not in my own room, hers is probably your best guess.'

She smiled. 'I'll knock.'

Jaghar nearly cursed. Demon be damned. Being the kind of man to lust after anyone even when he ought to be grieving was bad enough; did she really need to see it in his eyes too?

'Thanks,' he said.

He found Velvet in her room, sitting motionless in her windowsill under her old white blanket. She didn't turn around when he closed the hidden door behind him, her back towards him, her eyes staring away from him.

'Princess?'

She turned around so quickly she nearly lost her balance. 'Jaghar! Oh, thank the gods – where in the world have you been?'

Obvious relief, and yet voice sounded strangely hard, yet her smile was strangely stiff. A brave attempt to pretend nothing extraordinary was going on, that this was a conversation as usual, except that they both knew better.

He hesitated, then sank down on her bed. She followed him with her eyes, but didn't move to sit next to him.

'Madelena,' he said. 'And Emeric before her.'

'Emeric?'

At least when she was curious she still sounded like herself. He sighed and said, 'Wanted to know how the investigation was faring.'

'Oh, did he?'

Jaghar grimaced. 'Scared they'll go after him next, apparently.'

'Oh.' She scoffed. That, too, looked entirely authentic. 'Could have seen that coming. Bloody coward. What did you tell him?'

'Nothing,' Jaghar said, rubbing a hand over his face. 'If one of his pretty friends is behind this, I didn't want him to go blathering about what we might know or suspect.'

'And you didn't feel like doing him a favour?'

He gave her a thin smile. 'Admittedly.'

They were both silent for a moment. She sat staring out the window, a sharp silhouette against the stark blue sky. The amusement had seeped out of her again. Jaghar wanted to get up and take her in his arms, strip the black silk off her and tuck her into bed where no dukes or uncles could harass her – but she looked miles away from this room, miles away from him, too, and he'd rather lay his hands on burning iron than distress her even further.

'I went to see Father,' she finally said.

'You – just now?'

She nodded.

'Oh, gods, Velvet – you could have asked me to...'

'I wanted to go alone,' she said flatly, but she still didn't look his way, and her shoulders stiffened. 'It seemed – more fitting, I suppose.'

Jaghar clutched his fingers into the mattress, a hollow pit opening in his stomach – more *fitting*? Since when did she care about following courtly etiquette when there was no-one else around to see them anyway? Of course she could go alone if she felt strong enough to handle the sight of her own father's body by herself, but he knew the way she tensed up underneath her dress, and it rarely signalled she was doing fine.

Why in the world hadn't she just asked him? She should know he'd have abandoned his work within a heartbeat to come with her.

'Velvet, are you – alright?'

Ridiculous question. They both knew she wasn't. And yet the sarcastic answer he expected didn't come; instead she finally turned towards him and forced a smile that looked like a plea for help. 'Don't worry. I'm not collapsing.'

'No, but...'

'I'm *fine*, Jaghar.' Who was she trying to convince, after the night that orphaned her? 'It was strange to see him, but he really didn't even look like himself – I've been imagining more frightening sights for the entire night, and at least he seemed peaceful...'

She looked away again, her shoulders trembling. Jaghar opened his mouth and closed it again, lost for words. She clearly was about as fine as the average corpse was alive. But under normal circumstances she'd crawl into his arms and hide there until she dared to face the world again, not insist there was nothing wrong in the first place –

When in the world had she stopped trusting him?

He kicked off his boots and pulled his feet onto the bed. His thoughts were making desperate attempts to make sense of the world – why would she lie to him if she knew damn well that he'd see right through her pretences? Did she want him to ask more? She didn't make a habit of those games, and yet he'd rather believe that explanation than the only alternative his could come up with.

Was she angry? Disappointed with his failure to protect her father?

The pit in his stomach was a gaping crevice now. Don't run to dramatic conclusions, he tried to reassure himself. Of course she's reacting in unusual ways, she's never lost a father before – but she hadn't closed herself to him this way after Hrithik told her about the unknown threat to her father's life, or after the king of Redwood died a violent death at her table, or when she had been frightened of marrying Donovan...

The silence turned more deafening the longer it lasted. He swallowed his dread and steeled himself.

'Velvet?'

'Hm?'

'You seem to be a little more upset than you're telling me.'

She froze, then turned towards him and swung her legs off the windowsill, her green eyes wide and helpless. 'Please – I'm so sorry, I shouldn't be...'

'Demon's sake, there's nothing you should be. What is it?'

'I just couldn't stop thinking about it while I was standing there,' she burst out, and all the stiffness vanished. Suddenly she was a shivering, trembling mess in her dismal black dress, tears running over her cheeks as if they'd been waiting for the starting shot. 'I couldn't stop thinking – someone was killing him while we were *standing* there, Jaghar – we were making stupid small talk in a stupid garden and meanwhile someone walked into his room to stick a knife into his back, and I had no idea – I didn't know – if you'd just been with him...'

The rest of her sentence dissolved in a choked sob, smothered behind her hands over her face. Jaghar stared at her, his stomach turning. If he hadn't been standing in that stupid garden. If he'd just been where he should have been.

'I'm sorry,' she stammered, 'I'm so sorry, I didn't want to make a scene...'

'Velvet.' He closed his eyes. Shame burned a painful path through his chest. Not making a scene? Why was she trying to protect him from the consequences his own stupidity? 'Please, you're being a miracle already – it's not your job to—'

She jumped up before he could finish his sentence and fell down beside him on the bed, curling up against him to hide her teary face into his shirt. Jaghar folded his arms around her and pressed her against his chest. His mouth was dry as desert sand. It's not your job to prevent murders, he wanted to finish. I should have been there. He counted on me to keep him safe, and instead I was enjoying the good life by your side while someone was killing him in the plain light of day. I'm sorry. I failed you. But he didn't manage to part his lips; the shame clogged his throat, thick and heavy like clotting fat.

He held her. It was all he could do – hold her as if his arms could shield her from all pain and grief in the world, run his fingers through her dark curls and kiss the crown of her head until her breath finally slowed and the shivers subsided. Still she didn't move, cuddled up against him like an animal looking for shelter.

'Sorry,' she whispered, breathing warm air into his shirt.

'Stop apologising, Velvet.' He sighed. 'I still don't think you're a frail little princess, and I won't start thinking it either. No need for excuses.'

She uttered a choked laugh, or something like a laugh. 'But I'm collapsing half of the time and I don't even—'

'Yes, of course you are! And then what?'

'You *expect* me to run around like a crying mess?' She looked up, the fire flickering back to life in her eyes. 'And that's supposed to tell me I'm not some pathetic excuse of a princess?'

'No,' he said, closing his eyes for a heartbeat, 'that's supposed to tell you you're human, Velvet.'

'What?'

'Collapsing is what normal people do. Collapsing a little less is what the exceptionally tough do. Getting out of bed and trying to solve your own father's death mere hours after he was brutally murdered takes the kind of nerves I can barely wrap my head around, alright?'

'But *you* don't collapse! You're just doing what you have to do even if—'

'Princess.' He averted his gaze and sucked in a deep breath. 'Stop doing this to yourself. I didn't become this way because I *liked* it. Do you think I was anywhere near composed when I crawled out of that hell-hole in Shamouk?'

'No,' she whispered. 'No, but...'

'I've been living on hate and emptiness for a decade, Velvet. But you've seen what that made me. You've hated what it made me, and you were damn well right to. Could you stop trying to convince yourself that that's what you should aspire to be in life?'

She opened her mouth again, then closed it without a word, sank back against him, and pulled her knees to her chest.

'Oh.'

'So.' He closed his eyes and pressed the memories away, or at least made an attempt to. 'Stop apologising, stop thinking you should be something cold and soulless, and...'

'But I don't want to put everything on your shoulders either, Jaghar!'

'If I had too much on my shoulders it would be my own damn fault,' he said bitterly, and she froze in his arms.

'What?'

'Nothing. Never mind. Just...'

She sat up before he could finish his sentence. Even with his eyes shut he could feel her gaze on his face, warming his skin. Seeing too much. Knowing him too well, as always.

'Jaghar? You're not *blaming* yourself, are you?'

He sucked in a cold breath, looked up. She was staring at him with glistening green eyes, the sticky traces of tears still on her cheeks. No sense in denying it, he knew in that moment, no sense in trying to spare her the subject until she'd had a few weeks to gather her mind again – she wouldn't be fooled for a heartbeat.

'I should never have left him alone.'

She snorted. 'Neither should the rest of the castle.'

'He relied on *me* to keep him safe.' The words formed themselves on his lips, too loud and too sharp, thoughts that had been slumbering under the surface since the moment he found Trystan's body. 'You said it yourself – if I had just been there...'

'No, no, no.' She pulled away from his embrace, suddenly all determination, all agitation. 'That's not what I said at all. Don't start doing that again, taking responsibility for things that aren't your responsibility at all. You left him alone for five minutes so many times. You had absolutely no way to know this time would be different. Not being omniscient for once is not the same as being a murderer, alright?'

'No, but—'

'Jaghar, if you're to blame for following me into that garden, I'm to blame just as much for walking out with the intention to make you follow me. Do you want to call *me* a murderer?'

'He didn't pay *you* to keep him...'

'And do you really think he'd have blamed you?'

Jaghar opened his mouth, then closed it again. Through the haze of his thoughts, drawn on his mind's eye so sharply that it hurt, he could see the look on Trystan's face already – that calm smile, mild and reassuring. We all make mistakes, the king would have said. It's no more than human, don't worry too much about it. Let's just focus on what to do now, shall we?

He averted his face. Velvet lay her hand around his upper arm and pulled him closer, wrapping her arms around his shoulders as he sagged against her. Through the black silk the warmth of her body found him reassuring as always.

'All I was saying,' she said quietly, 'is that I wish we would have known. Not that you should have known. You've been away for months, you barely even returned to work yet – and you're not blaming Madelena for overlooking the threat either, are you?'

He groaned. 'Must you be so bloody convincing?'

'It's easy to be convincing when I'm right,' she said wryly. 'Good gods, Spymaster, you stepped into a *garden* for two minutes. It's not as if you kindly opened the door for the murderer and showed him the way to that bloody room. You have no reason to blame yourself.'

She sounded so reassuringly sure of herself. So unmovable, so determined. He clung to that tone like a drowning man – no reason to blame himself. A sentence sounding like a lie, but a lie he wanted to believe so, so badly. And if *she* could believe it, perhaps even he could manage if he kept trying long enough...

A shiver ran through him. No reason to blame himself. Don't start doing that again. Slowly the knots in his stomach untangled themselves, even if the sharp stings of loss didn't soften. With a muffled groan he grabbed her hand and pulled it to his lips, pressing a kiss to her knuckles. Her hold on his torso didn't weaken.

'Did I tell you how much I love you?' he muttered.

A small chuckle. 'I think you mentioned something once or twice.'

'Velvet...' He pulled himself from the safety of her embrace and laid a hand around her pale face, wiping the last tears off her cheek with his thumb. From so close the moss green of her eyes glittered like summer leaves in the sun. 'There is no once or twice with you. There's just forever. Whatever happens – whatever you put on my shoulders. Will you please remember that from now on?'

She nodded. New tears were welling up in her eyes, but this time she didn't avert her gaze.

'Will you stop blaming yourself for things you could never have known, then?'

He sighed. 'Will try.'

'You'd better try your best,' she said wryly, and he managed a smile.

'That's an order, I suppose?'

She gave him a watery smile in return. 'Oh, definitely.'

'Well. That settles it, then.'

They both chuckled quietly, then sat next to each other in silence for a long minute, hands intertwined in the blankets between them. It was a silence that nearly made Jaghar forget that time was still turning, that the world outside this room still existed, that there was still a war to be won in his own home...

He muttered a curse as the thought emerged again. Velvet threw him a quick glance, concern gleaming in her eyes.

'Work?'

'Everything,' he said, suppressing a next curse. 'Do you mind having a word on practical...'

'No, of course.' She veered up. 'Anything I can do?'

'Depends on where we stand. Madelena told me you've been speaking with Wymond?'

'Oh, yes,' she said, taking a deep breath. 'Looks like we have one vote, at least. And I had a word with Reginald, and he'll testify for the Council. That's all, but...'

'That's *all*?' He didn't fully manage to suppress his incredulous grin as his heart made a sudden, hopeful leap. 'You got more work done than I did, Princess.'

She sent him another feeble smile. 'Madelena – did she find anything already about – about...'

'Nothing concrete. I need to go have a word with a few people myself.' Foreign diplomats tended to show a remarkable memory improvement when confronted with his more persuasive glares, he had found over the years. 'But I'm starting to believe that whoever made use of this – opportunity...'

He faltered for a moment. Velvet gave him a stern look.

'This opportunity for which you are *not* to blame.'

'Still trying very hard to believe that.' He rubbed his eyes. 'Whoever is behind this – I'm starting to believe they know more about our security measures than I'd want them too. It's damn near impossible to *accidentally* remain unseen like that. So I'll have the service ask around in that direction, but of course the problem is...'

'If someone knew where your spies were posted, they may as well know about the true intentions of the service?'

'In theory, yes.'

She groaned. 'That's not helping at all.'

'No.'

Again they were both quiet for a moment, a silence of calculations, of considerations. Then Velvet slowly said, 'If you need a silly princess to have a word with anyone...'

He managed a smile. 'Yes. Will let you know. I think you mostly need to deal with a host of dukes for now, though.'

'I know,' she said, pulling a face. 'Aldred should be arriving soon. Haven't seen him since I was fourteen and he told me that my narrow hips would be an unhelpful asset in the search for a husband, so I'm sure that will be a lovely reunion.'

Jaghar snorted a laugh. 'Demon's sake. I've clearly been setting the wrong priorities all this time.'

'Oh, yes – you should obviously have taken hip measurements before you even started *thinking* about marriage.' Her smile turned brighter, for the first time that day. 'Too late now, Spymaster. You're stuck with me and my narrow skeleton, I'm afraid.'

'A mistake that will likely haunt me for the rest of my life.'

'You can certainly rely on the mistake to do so, yes,' she said dryly, and he heaved his most dramatic sigh.

'Well. I'll just have to live with it.'

She flung herself into his arms, pressing him back in her blankets with a giggle that lifted the weight on his heart for a miraculous, blissful moment. He managed to restrain himself for four, five heartbeats as she climbed over him to press a dozen kisses to his forehead and his cheeks and his nose, more and more determined with every next one; then he broke and burst out laughing, rolling her over to kiss her back.

'Hmm,' she muttered against his lips, with a satisfied moan he felt in every inch of his body. 'Something tells me you won't have *that* much trouble accepting your unlucky fate, Spymaster.'

He raised an eyebrow. 'I might—'

Her kiss smothered the rest of that sentence – a deep, wild kiss that knocked the breath out of him and submerged him into that little world only the two of them shared, a world of soft hands and flowery perfume, a world in which death and danger didn't exist. He groaned and wrapped his arms around her to draw her closer, burying his fingers in the satin of her hair. For a few impossible moments he could forget the hollow grief that burned in him, the questions he couldn't answer, the Council and the votes to win. Her frail body against him was all that mattered, and the quiet moans he drew from her under his lips...

Outside, trumpets blared.

Velvet stiffened in his arms, then muttered a dazed curse and pulled away from him. 'Aldred.'

'Never liked him much,' Jaghar said, drawing her back against him. She let out a muffled laugh into his shirt.

'Jaghar...'

'I know, I know.' Votes. Opinions. Secrets. All the nonsense he never wanted to think about again. Forcing his frustration back he sat up, lifted her into his lap, and quickly tucked a few wild curls back into place. Outside the courtyard quickly filled up with voices, the court gathering to welcome yet another nobleman; he saw the exhaustion rise on Velvet's face again at the sound alone.

'You'll manage this part, Princess,' he muttered, kissing her forehead a last time. 'Keep your head high. Keep your shoulders straight. Even if all you do for the rest of this day is surviving – you'll be doing enough, I promise.'

She drew in a deep breath. 'When do I see you?'

'I'll be here tonight. As early as I can manage.'

A last nod, a last kiss, and she hurried out of the room, ready to welcome yet another duke to Rock Hall.

CHAPTER 7

J aghar sneaked into her room at midnight, just as the muffled blaring of trumpets signalled the change of guards on the courtyard below.

The tension in his movements told Viviette he was as exhausted as she was. Yet he checked the locks of her doors and windows before he even turned to the bed where she lay curled up under the heavy blankets, wide awake as she had been since her maid had convinced her to at least make an *attempt* at sleeping hours ago. In the last glow of the embers, his eyes were dark as a starless night, his face a wall of shadows.

'Velvet?' A cautious whisper as he sank down on the edge of the mattress. 'Did I wake you?'

'Couldn't sleep,' she mumbled.

He sighed and began to unbutton his shirt. Her eyes seemed glued to the quick, seasoned movements of his slender fingers, the muscular ridges of his abdomen emerging from under the dark linen – a sight so comforting, so familiar, that it somehow silenced the worst of her reeling thoughts. She wanted to sit up and pull him closer. She wanted to undress him like she would have done any other night. But after the exhausting eternity of this evening, even lifting her hands seemed an impossible effort, and she lay unmoving until he eventually slipped underneath the blankets as well and rested his head in the pillows to face her. His body was close enough to feel the warmth of it. Still he didn't touch her.

'How are you feeling?' he said quietly.

'Drained.'

A sigh. 'Yes.'

All other nights she'd have asked questions. Would have wanted to know about the state of the investigation, the clues, the suspicions. Now she could barely muster the energy to say, 'Did anything happen?'

'Some conversations.' His voice was flat with tiredness. 'Nothing of use. Got a little unpleasant with the fellows from the Higher Riverlands.'

Her guts cramped. 'And?'

'Would be very surprised if it turns out they know more than they told me. Don't think it's been Donovan. Then again...'

He closed his eyes for a moment, and didn't finish his sentence. Viviette swallowed.

'We don't know who else it might have been either?'

'No.'

Again they lay in silence for a few minutes, until he eventually moved up half an inch and added, 'How was your evening? I saw you speak with Aldred?'

'I still don't think he likes me much,' she said numbly. The old duke had barely been speaking with her, really. He had mostly spoken *at* her, in croaking monologues on the many responsibilities of a noble lady which she suspected to have been subtle suggestions she should just have stayed at Donovan's court. 'And Gideon continues to ignore me.'

'And Eluard? He arrived just before dinner, didn't he?'

'Was pretty pleasant. Then again, he was pretty pleasant with Emeric too.' As a matter of fact, the young duke had given the impression he would be pleasant even with the Empress herself.

Jaghar sighed. 'Well.'

'They said Laudine would be here tonight,' she added quietly. 'Couldn't really bring up the energy to wait.'

'Of course.' He hesitated for a moment, then added, 'Enough time to have a word with her and the others tomorrow.'

Viviette closed her eyes for a heartbeat, and nodded. Have a word. The notion alone seemed utterly useless, with the memory of Aldred's dry disapproval still at the forefront of her mind – she had tried being clever, charming, understanding, and all he had seemed to want was for her to simply be quiet. What if the others wouldn't be any better – what if Osric and Gerald would arrive tomorrow and look straight past her like Gideon had done... What was the sense in having *words* if she was hardly allowed to even open her mouth?

'And if I can't convince them?' she managed, her voice too small.

You can convince them, he should have said. Of course you can. Of course they'll listen to what you have to tell them, see who you are, see what you can do. But she saw it in the lines on his face before he opened his mouth – that the hours of fruitless efforts had left him as drained as they had left her.

'I really don't know, Velvet.'

Her limbs seemed paralysed, the weight of mountains pressing on her chest. Inches away from her Jaghar closed his eyes, a small muscle twitching at the corner of his lips.

'Oh,' she whispered.

'I don't know how to find that murderer,' he added, still in that same eerily empty tone. 'I don't know what clues I'm overlooking. I don't know what I'll tell the Council if we don't solve the case in two nights. I don't know – anything, honestly.'

She swallowed. But you always know everything. You always work out everything. Yet none of those hollow statements seemed to carry any meaning now; nothing she could say would take that impossible weight from his heart. How had she ever done that, taking any weight of his heart? She barely even remembered how to talk.

But he was so close...

Holding her breath, she moved her hand a few inches and found the hard muscles of his shoulders under her fingertips, tense enough to feel like steel under his skin. The soft sound of his breathing caught at the same moment.

'Velvet?'

'Sorry,' she breathed. 'I just don't know what to say.'

Then his arms were around her – warm, strong arms, pulling her against his naked body as if nothing would ever be wrong in the world again.

And at once she understood him again. At once he made sense to her mind again, the tender certainty of his touches, the safety of his strength as he wrapped her into his embrace and pressed his lips against her forehead... Her hands found their way over his body out of sheer habit, along the sculpted lines of his stomach and the slender muscles of his back. A body she knew as well as her own, deadly like a weapon and strong like a lion – and still hers, still entirely, undeniably hers.

He let out a moan when she ran her nails along his spine, that soft, stifled moan of a pleasure he wouldn't allow himself to feel. 'Velvet...'

She came up to kiss him before he could say more – every next word could only ruin this moment of sudden harmony, and all she wanted was for the world to be easy for a few blissful minutes. She found his mouth without hesitation even in the darkness. Jaghar kissed her back like a starving man, drowning her in the musky smell of his body, the salty taste of his lips. Around her the world dissolved into a fog of nothingness. His touch was all she knew, his fingers clawing into her body, his lips trailing over her jaw and neck and pressing kiss after kiss onto her tingling skin...

All she knew, and all she wanted.

She dug her fingers into his shoulders and wrapped her right leg around his hip to press herself tighter against his naked body. Between her legs his arousal jolted, and his heavy breath again faltered for the blink of an eye. Then his kisses returned, lips sucking and nibbling as they made their way down over her body, along her neck, her shoulder, her collarbone. Up the slope of her breast. He closed his lips around her nipple and teased his tongue over the sensitive tip until a moan escaped her. His quiet chuckle was the world's most reassuring sound – that chuckle he had given her so many times before, when he brought her to a screaming climax in the forests of Redwood or lifted her before him in the saddle to press her against him even on the road –

When everything had been easy.

But nothing seemed complicated now, as he trailed down along her belly and drowned her skin in the sensations of his warm breath and the rough stubble of his jaws. Nothing was complicated at least about the shameless desire in his soft moans, about the wet warmth his caresses roused between her legs. Their bodies understood each other even with their minds in disarray, and all else melted from her thoughts under the haze of this old, familiar need for him. He loved her. He wanted her. The rest was secondary, a mere temporary disruption, nothing that couldn't be solved. She closed her eyes. He dug his strong fingers into her thighs to move them apart, and cold night air found the vulnerable wetness in between...

Fists pounded on her bedroom door, hurried and urgent.

Jaghar shot up, squeezing her thighs so tightly she nearly yelped. For a few heartbeats the knocking subsided and they sat frozen between her rumpled blankets, fear and arousal fighting for preference in Viviette's throat. Then again the fists landed against the door, and Jaghar snatched his ivory knife and trousers off the floor with a muffled curse.

'Expecting anyone?' he hissed.

'No, but – nobody knows you're here, do they? Or—'

'Your Highness?' Madelena's urgent voice called from the corridor.

The last traces of her arousal vanished from her mind at once. Viviette jumped from the bed and pulled her nearest dress from the floor – why in the world would Madelena need her, or Jaghar, or anyone at all, at this hour of the night?

'A minute!' she yelled.

She was even faster; Jaghar was still pulling his shirt over his head when she turned the key in her lock. Madelena burst into the room in a flood of yellow torchlight, the bags under her eyes all the more visible with the shadows playing over her face. Her eyes shot to the other side of the room at once and didn't show a trace of surprise when she found Jaghar beside the bed.

'There you are – thank the gods.'

'What in the world happened?' Viviette threw the door shut and turned around as her hazy, tangled thoughts ran past the options – a fire? A Taavi attack? Duelling dukes? 'Nobody *died*, I hope?'

A grim darkness slid over Madelena's face. 'Very sorry, Your Highness.'

'What – who?'

'Reginald is dead.'

Viviette stared at her. Her mind scrambled to make sense of the words – Reginald. Dead. Their meaning was clear, yes, but their implications...

Behind her, Jaghar recovered in an instant. 'What happened?'

'Not clear yet,' Madelena said, sinking down in a chair at the hearth without invitation. A smear of ink ran over her left cheek, Viviette noted only now. 'Laudine arrived at Rock Hall half an hour ago. Wanted to wake him to say hello. Found him stabbed to death under the blankets of his own bed.'

The silence was deafening and lasted too long. The air in Viviette's lungs thinned as she desperately tried to keep breathing, to look normal and composed – Reginald. Stabbed to death. A young nobleman of impeccable character, with no unpleasant history as far as anyone knew – and Jaghar must have been thorough before the man had been hired as her father's personal secretary. No reason why any Taavi Empresses or Riverland kings would want *him* dead. Which left only one possible motive...

'This – this is about me, isn't it?'

The words sounded strangely cold from her own lips. Madelena closed her eyes, the lack of sleep suddenly very visible on her face. Jaghar muttered a curse as he sank down on the edge of the bed; when Viviette turned around, she found nothing but hard, sharp determination on his face.

'If it isn't about you,' he said, 'this must be the most unfortunate series of events in history.'

Viviette slowly sank down into the remaining chair and buried her face in her arms, the world turning around her – about *her*. Because of *her*. There was no other sensible explanation. Somehow someone knew about her father's plan to make her his heir, someone desperate enough to kill a king to prevent it from happening. Two dead – because of *her*.

'Do I need to go take a look?' Jaghar's voice sounded strangely unaffected against the whirlwind crashing through her thoughts. Nothing like the man who had kissed her so tenderly moments ago. 'If there are any traces—'

'Already did,' Madelena interrupted him, followed by the sound of a notebook pulled open. 'He must have died about four hours ago, not long after sunset. Looks like the killer surprised him in his sleep, so I suppose he or she showed up shortly after Reginald went to bed.'

'He or she?' Jaghar repeated. The tone of his voice suggested he was raising an eyebrow.

'Coming at that. Murder looks rather different from the one on the king. That was – pardon me the details, Your Highness...'

Viviette hastily looked up. 'No, please, go on.'

'The king's murder,' Madelena continued, unfazed, 'looked like it was committed by someone who knew how to handle a weapon. Single stab, with the right amount of force. No hesitation, apparently. Whereas Reginald...' She wiped a loose lock away from her face. 'Seven stab wounds all over his torso. None of them very deep. As if someone who never held a knife before decided to commit a murder and just – went loose. Not a person with a lot of physical strength. Which is why I thought it may as well be a woman.'

Viviette nearly gagged. In her mind she could see a cloaked silhouette bent over the bed, blood drops spattering around as the intruder butchered the young man lying under the blankets with mindless, unhinged violence. Reginald – poor, poor Reginald, who had all but cried about her father that morning, who had been so relieved about the chance to help her...

And instead – she had killed him?

'Any idea how the murderer came in?' Jaghar said, his voice still frighteningly business-like.

'Door was unlocked, according to Laudine.'

'Why wouldn't he lock his door before he went to sleep?'

'No idea – he may have he expected someone?' Madelena shrugged. 'Although he was naked – that would be strange. Not the type for late night visits of indecent nature, I'd say.'

Neither of them seemed to have an answer to the silence that fell. Viviette clenched her hands and started, 'But...'

'Yes, Your Highness?'

'Regardless of the question who killed Reginald,' she said, and tried not to sound as frightened as she felt. 'If we agree he was killed because of the succession issue – because someone doesn't want me on the throne for some reason – then that someone needs to have *known* about my father's plan, yes? And that same person must have known that Reginald knew about it as well. There would be no reason to kill him otherwise.'

Dead. Because of her. Because of some objection to her position she couldn't even understand herself. Two men in two days – dead.

'In theory,' Jaghar said slowly, 'it's possible that someone heard about the king's plans through Reginald. In which case Reginald might even have been killed to make sure he wouldn't let us know who he told.'

'He said he didn't tell anyone.'

'Then admitted he wrote Laudine. What if he had another secret up his sleeve?'

Viviette buried her face in her hands. What if? Somehow it was a reassuring thought – if Reginald had lied about his contacts, at least it wouldn't be her fault he died –

But he had looked so genuinely shocked, and so genuinely embarrassed at even his innocent letter to his aunt.

'He really didn't look like he had,' she muttered. 'I know I can't be sure, but it seems very, very unlikely to me, honestly.'

Jaghar sighed and averted his face. 'Well. Let's assume he spoke the truth, then. Your intuition is frighteningly accurate, generally speaking.'

Madelena's face suggested she'd be very happy to ask a number of things, but she stayed silent until Jaghar eventually looked up.

'Madelena? Is there anyone else the king may have seen that day without us noticing?'

'Hardly likely. He spoke with Reginald, he had a meeting about river rights where inheritance questions weren't relevant in any way, and a meeting with Kusti where he won't have mentioned anything of value, let alone this. I don't see any room for slipped secrets.'

'And just after dinner?'

Madelena shook her head. 'In theory he may have received spontaneous visitors, told them about the idea and accidentally given them a motive for murder – I had nobody on him in that hour after dinner because you'd be speaking with him anyway. But it does sound rather unlikely, wouldn't you say?'

Another silence. Jaghar averted his face.

'But if we didn't tell anyone,' Viviette said, 'and Father didn't tell anyone—'

Her breath caught in her throat. Then what else do you want to suggest, she wanted to say, that someone lay listening behind the curtains during that conversation? Stood with his ear against the door? But the ridiculous suggestion reminded her of a memory not nearly so ridiculous – she *had* thought for a moment, as she talked with her father, that Jaghar was listening along –

Because the tapestry had moved.

The *tapestry* had moved.

'Princess?'

Only now did she realise she had jolted up. Jaghar was studying her, a slight frown on his sharp face, his eyes black as ink.

'Someone – someone may have been listening along,' she managed.

'What?'

'When I spoke with him. After you two left.' Her blood was rushing in her ears all of a sudden. How in the world had something so important slipped her mind? 'I remember – I thought for a moment someone stood in the secret corridor – because the tapestry moved a little – but you said it wasn't you and I entirely forgot about it again. I'm so sorry – I hadn't realised...'

Jaghar stared at her as if she'd spoken in another language. He didn't move. He barely even blinked. Viviette swallowed and added, 'I don't know—'

'None of our people was there,' Madelena said, her voice still so composed that it could only be theatre. 'I didn't post anyone near, at least – and if anyone was around by accident, the reports would have mentioned it.'

Another silence. Jaghar still sat frozen on the edge of the bed, looking straight past her, his eyes cold and expressionless. Madelena was frowning at her notebook, the confusion obvious on even her face.

Viviette swallowed the sour gall rising in her throat. 'But then – is there anyone else who knows about those corridors?'

Jaghar cursed.

He stood so quickly she nearly jolted backwards in her chair. With four steps he was at the door. Only then did she find her voice back, but even his name sounded shrill and shocked on her lips; when he turned around with his hand on the doorknob, the look in his eyes made her wish she'd never called out for him at all.

'Jaghar – what in the world—'

'Be careful, Velvet.' It came out sharp and breathless. 'Be very, very damned careful until I'm sure if – Madelena, keep a look on everything around her. Secret doors, too. I'm back in a few hours to discuss the rest.'

'But what...'

'I've been an idiot again,' he snapped, and vanished into the shadows of the night.

CHAPTER 8

To think that he had once believed he'd never set a foot onto Mine Street again.

The houses passed him by on a blur as he strode past the seemingly endless row of pubs, gambling sheds and whorehouses – whiffs of beer and piss and vomit, shreds of drunken bawling, a woman's voice moaning and groaning through an open window above him. Jaghar didn't even remember in what unseemly establishment he had tried to drink away the pain of Velvet's absence months ago. All these places looked identical anyway – except for that one house his thoughts focussed on now.

Please don't let it be true, part of his mind was begging. Please don't let me have been this much of a fool – but with every hurried footstep the thought that had hit him like an ice-cold lightning bolt made more sense to him. Opportunity, yes. Motive, possibly...

But if it was true – then what did it make of him?

He didn't bother knocking when he finally reached the house with the stag's head at the far end of the street. Under the soles of his boots, the lock gave in with two well-aimed kicks; the door slammed open and allowed entrance to the rickety but spotless hallway he'd never wanted to see again in his life. In the room to his left a woman's voice started screaming alarm. He ran upstairs before she could come out and hinder him. Around him the house woke up in shocked cries and shrill warnings, and none of it reached his ears. He saw only that single door at the top of the stairs, and swung it open without slowing down.

It wasn't locked.

A few coals still glowed in the hearth. Enough to distinguish the contours of the room in the dark – the narrow window, the low bed. The shape moving in that same bed, a head of red curls coming up and freezing a few inches above the pillow.

He had his hands around Rosin's shoulders the next moment, dragging her from the blankets and slamming her back against the thin wall. Only then did she cry out in useless, belated shock, her voice mingling with the chorus of panicking women crying murder and alarm outside the room. In her thin nightdress she was shivering. Shock, yes. Fear, perhaps. But even with his face inches away from hers, he couldn't detect a trace of surprise in her eyes.

At that moment, he knew he was right.

A strange coldness washed over him, spreading from the core of his bones to the tips of his fingers until he barely felt her trembling shoulders under his hands anymore. Behind him the crying voices had found the ruined lock. He could hear the bravest of them approach the room already – 'Rosin? *Rosin*?'

'Tell them to piss off,' he hissed.

She cowered against the wall but shrieked, 'It's alright! Friend of mine!'

The footsteps outside halted. Feverish voices exchanged whispers on the stairs. Then a stern woman's voice snapped, 'Don't let him leave without paying for the door unless you want to repair it yourself, yes?'

'Yes – yes, I'll get it fixed!'

They removed themselves, muttering furious complaints as they retreated into their bedrooms again. Rosin sucked in a shivering breath, then shrieked when Jaghar clawed his hands around her arms even tighter. 'Ow! What in the world—'

'Don't play stupid.' His voice was a hoarse growl. 'You were in Rock Hall the day before yesterday, correct?'

She opened her eyes wider. 'I – I—'

'Are you going to lie to me?'

She swallowed but shook her head. He held her as if to squeeze the blood from her arms now.

'You listened to Trystan as he spoke with his daughter. You were there in the corridor behind the tapestry.'

'I – *Jaghar*! You're hurting—'

'Yes,' he hissed, 'and I'll be hurting you much, *much* more if I find out you've been lying to me, so be wise and answer my questions. Did you listen to them?'

She nodded, her eyes wide enough to see the white around her irises now.

'Why?'

'I – I was just curious.'

'Just curious?' He bit out a joyless laugh. 'Were you trying to find me?'

Again she nodded.

'And then you stayed to listen after I left.' He barely suppressed a curse. 'And then? Who did you tell?'

'I didn't—'

'Didn't tell anyone? And I'm supposed to believe that, after someone stabbed a knife into Trystan's back a few hours later?'

'I swear I didn't kill—'

'And Reginald?'

Her mouth clapped shut.

The anger didn't so much come over him as break free within him – tore through the last reins of his self-restraint with red-hot rage and sent his hand flying to the knife at his belt. Seven shallow knife stabs. Sneaked into the room through the corridors, unlocked the door and killed the boy in his own bed like an animal to be slaughtered – and then there was the blade in Trystan's back...

'Jaghar, no – *please*!' Her voice rose to its shrillest heights. 'I'll tell you! I'll tell you what happened – please don't...'

His fingers froze around the ivory hilt of his knife. Gall burned in the back of his throat. He *wanted* to see her bleed like Trystan had bled, in a haze of bloodlust that frightened him as much as it frightened her – wanted to see her suffer to death at his feet like Reginald had suffered in the darkness of his own room. He wanted her to hurt like she had hurt Velvet, every gruelling, painful moment of it. But if he took his revenge...

She hadn't killed Trystan. She had, at least, not stuck the knife between his shoulder blades. If he gave in to the urges of his trembling hands, he might never find out who had.

'Fine,' he snapped, releasing his knife again. His hands were cold and sweaty. 'Tell me.'

'Only if you—'

"*Tell me.*'

She shrunk back against the wall, her eyes shooting from his face to the door and back. 'He said he'd make her his heir. That she could marry anyone she wanted. Then he mentioned you.' A scornful grin grew around her lips, breaking through the fear for a moment. 'He still didn't know, did he? Didn't notice you were fucking her straight under his—'

'Careful,' Jaghar growled, and the grin slid off her face again.

'I left after she left the room – then I mentioned it to a few people, nobody in...'

He drew his knife. Rosin shrieked and tried to pull away from him, then froze when he pressed the blunt side of the ivory blade against her throat. His hand shook with mindless fury.

'I damn well hope you have something more specific for me, Rosin.'

'I...'

'I know you're not stupid. You knew she'd have married me, given the chance.' A sting of cold grief stabbed through him. She would have, yes, and then the world had gone incomprehensibly mad. Then he had... What had he *done*? 'Am I to believe you shrugged and went home?'

She was breathing in short, faltering gasps under his blade. 'Please...'

'Should have fucking thought of that earlier, Rosin. What – did – you – do?'

Her eyes squeezed shut, she whispered, 'I – I told Emeric.'

The air turned to ice in his lungs. For a heartbeat he could only stare at her as the words rang through his head, louder and louder with each turn – told Emeric. Told *Emeric*. Even his fingers had forgotten how to move the knife against her throat.

Told Emeric.

What had she expected Trystan's brother to do? Smile and shrug? No, she'd picked him with the clear expectation that he would do something about the matter – keep Velvet off her own bloody throne, convince Trystan to make her marry anyway...

A joyless laugh fell over his lips, cutting as the knife between his fingers.

'How dare you. How dare you—'

'What should I have done, then!' she spit. 'Leave it to her to ruin your life? She's not going to make you happy, Jaghar, I *know* she could never make you happy – you don't need that little bitch to...'

His free fist shot forward and hit her against the temple, slamming the back of her head into the thin wood of the wall. She wavered on her feet. Jaghar pulled back his knife and took a step backwards – kill her, his mind screamed at him, kill her for seeing the life you could have had and ruining it with a single secret. But a corpse couldn't tell him the rest of the tale. He couldn't arrest Emeric to force the truth out of him, and at the very least Velvet should know the full story of her father's death.

Hell be damned. How was he going to tell her any of this? At the thought alone he wanted to crumble on the spot. Oh, remember that deranged woman who's been obsessed with me for years? That woman I allowed into the castle for far too long, who I personally showed around in the network, who I threw out without bothering to keep an eye on her? Turns out she killed your father just because of me...

Rosin slowly shuffled backwards, away from him. He shook off his brooding, with another sting of dread, and raised his knife in a simple, wordless warning. More wasn't needed to make her freeze again.

'What did you say to Emeric?'

'Only that Trystan wanted to pass him by – I swear that's all.'

Jaghar closed his eyes for a heartbeat. Only that Trystan wanted to pass him by. And then Emeric would have ambled into his brother's study and rammed a knife into his back at the first unguarded moment? It couldn't be that simple. His spies had gone over Emeric's ways, and if he remembered Madelena's summaries correctly, the prince hadn't left his room at all.

'How did he kill Trystan?'

Rosin hesitated a fraction too long, creeping away from the wall. 'I don't know.'

'I thought I warned you not to lie to me.'

'I – I suppose he just – I don't know, walked into the room and – I didn't see him anymore after I told him—'

'You're hiding something from me, Rosin.' He clenched his fingers around his knife. 'Last chance. How did he kill—'

'The secret corridors,' she blurted out.

'The – how did he know?' The world was reeling around him. 'Did you *show* him?'

'Well – I...'

With a growl Jaghar jumped forward and grabbed the collar of her nightdress to drag her back against the wall. His hand came up by its own volition, swinging the knife down without a single other thought. Damn the duty, damn the laws – she had killed his king, Velvet's father, in all ways except for the deadly stab itself –

'I can help you!' she shrieked. Just in time. The ivory point held still just inches away from the white, defenceless skin of her throat.

'I don't need your—'

'Oh, you know better.' A bitter, hateful grimace lay on her face now. She was trying to twist her way out of his grip, but he didn't yield an inch, didn't lower the knife before her face. 'They're going to crown him, Jaghar. You won't be able to accuse him of murder after the Council has made him king. So if you want to stop him before that time, you're going to need someone to tell the dukes what he's done.'

Cold, bitter hate spiralled through him as he stared at her triumphant face, her messy red curls, her body showing through the linen of her nightdress. He *touched* that body. The gall rose in his throat at the thought alone – he had fucked this monster, spent hours of her life in her bed, brought himself to believe he loved her, and now, after she betrayed him in the worst way possible, he was supposed to let her help him? He was supposed to *trust* her?

'Why would you,' he said hoarsely. 'You know it won't bring me back to you. I'd rather die than go back to you. Do you really want me to believe you'd suddenly help me achieve exactly what you wanted to prevent badly enough to kill a king for it?'

'Oh, no.' A grin grew on her face, a wolfish sneer. 'I never said I'd help you marry her. I know better. You'll be grateful when you see—'

'Shut *up*, will you?'

'I'll help you make Emeric lose the Council,' she said, shaking her curls over her shoulder with a dangerous smile up at him. As if she was in control again – and worse, perhaps she was. 'They can crown her, as far as I'm concerned.'

'Then...'

'But you'll marry me before the Council meets.'

Jaghar was vaguely aware he had lowered his knife. He couldn't care to raise it again. Marry her – *marry* her? Again the gall came up in the back of his throat. He didn't even want to spend a minute more than necessary in this damned room. The thought of spending a lifetime bound to her, even if it was only by a name in the Temple archives...

'You've gone mad.'

'Sure.' She scowled. 'Then kill me. Good luck getting your pretty princess back after Emeric marries her off to one his friends.'

For the bloody demon's sake. She *knew* the man. She had listened along with the conversations in Rock Hall for years and spent way too many of those evenings sharing in his gossip on the castle's inhabitants. Emeric would be happy to get rid of his niece indeed, and then what was he supposed to do?

Somehow the bastard should be stopped before his coronation. And all he could do –

Marry Rosin. Before the Council meeting.

Some of the mist cleared up in his head. Before the Council meeting. That gave him at least some more time to reconsider his options – until tomorrow night, at least. Twenty-four hours to find a way out of this rat trap. A better chance at least than killing her now and trying to convince the dukes of Emeric's guilt without a single witness or piece of evidence – within a day.

He averted his face. 'Fine.'

'What?'

'We have a deal.' He had to force the words over his lips, and the contents of his stomach nearly came out with them. Marry her? Was he really promising to marry *her*, barely a day after he'd still believed Velvet might be his within months? But what other option did he have at this moment? 'I'll see you tomorrow morning. You'll do exactly what I tell you to do. If you're successful...'

'You'll marry me?' She sounded hungry, and again he nearly gagged.

'Sunrise before the Council meeting.'

'Romantic,' she murmured, then jolted back when she saw his look and added, 'Alright, alright, I won't—'

'I bloody well wouldn't advise you to,' he snapped. 'Say one word too many and I might slit your throat anyway.'

'Oh, that's alright,' she said and smiled a strangely genuine smile at him. 'You'll realise how lucky you are soon enough. If I hadn't fought for you—'

She abruptly stopped talking when he turned his back towards her, his fingers still cramped around the hilt of his knife. Lucky. Fought for him – for *him*. Arranged Trystan's death for him, butchered Reginald for him. Hell's sake, how would anyone in Rock Hall ever forgive him, let alone...

'Wait for me tomorrow,' he managed, and fled the room, slamming the door behind him.

Mine Street was a blur. He stumbled off without seeing much, kicked a toothless drunk aside and disappeared into the first alley he could find, away from the watchful eyes of the gamblers and the whores. The darkness wrapped itself around him like a comforting hug, a reassuring blanket of invisibility – and yet nothing could reassure him when he sank down in the sand with his back against a wooden wall and curled his knees to his chest.

Marry Rosin.

Marry Rosin.

There had to be some way out. He had to find some way to make her uphold her end of the deal without obliging him to go through with this madness. If not for himself, then at least for Velvet –

Velvet.

She'd have to know. He had to tell her that she'd lost her father because he couldn't handle the obsessions of a whore he had brought into the castle himself. That her uncle committed a murder only to prevent them from marrying. That he promised himself to the woman who single-handedly caused all this misery.

And then she'd know –

Kindly opened the door for the murderer and showed him the way to that bloody room...

His stomach recoiled. He barely had the time to jump to his feet and bent over before the sickness made its way up his throat, driven by the thought of the pain in those green eyes, the disappointment he couldn't save her from. He threw up like an old drunk in the gutter, shivering and shuddering, and on the verge of crying.

CHAPTER 9

'**Y**our Highness?'

The servant's voice cut through her frightened thoughts. Viviette tore her gaze away from the hall's entrance, where Jaghar still hadn't appeared even hours after sunrise, and tried to swallow her fears down. He knew what he was doing. He always knew what he was doing. He had to be safe – but where in the world had he *gone*?

'What is it?'

'Prince Emeric asks to speak with you, Your Highness. Immediately, please.'

Viviette blinked. Immediately. Emeric was no higher in rank than she was; he had no right to demand her presence, let alone immediately. But what was the sense in objecting purely to make a point? She would only antagonise him and draw unpleasant attention to herself – and until Jaghar returned she had nothing else to do anyway.

'Thank you,' she said, standing up from her meagre, unfinished breakfast. 'Where do I find him?'

'The garden, Your Highness.'

The *garden*? Did he believe she would be in the mood for a refreshing morning walk?

'Thank you,' she said, standing up. 'I'll go see him.'

From the corners of her eyes she saw Madelena's men get to their feet on both sides of the hall. Ready to follow her wherever she would go, not only through the public part of the castle, but through the hidden corridors surrounding them as well...

Why in the world had he added that instruction to the list before he stormed out last night? *Had* anyone been listening along with her and her father? But who in the world could know about the corridors if even her father hadn't known about them until Jaghar found them again?

She threw a last glance at the entrance of the hall as she turned towards the garden doors. Still not a glimpse of his silver-blond hair. What was he *doing*? Even Madelena had looked stunned at his brusque departure, and neither of them had been able to come up with a decent explanation for that fluttering tapestry –

He wouldn't be doing anything reckless, would he?

Her feet walked her outside without consulting her conscious thoughts, into the fresh air of this mild summer morning, smelling of roses and raspberries. She swallowed away the bitter memories as she made her way over the meandering paths she had walked so often with her father, forcing polite smiles at all knights and nobles enjoying the morning sun. Emeric's dark-haired head was nowhere to be seen. Only at the far end of the garden did she catch the sound of his voice, coming from behind an elegant arbour covered in thorny roses, and accompanied by another male voice she didn't recognise at once. The next sound to welcome her was a resounding burst of laughter.

Laughter.

She didn't know how she managed to hold onto her unmoving mask when she found Gideon sitting beside her uncle on a low granite bench, wiping tears of mirth from his eyes. Emeric himself sat lounging back in the same bench, one foot resting on the edge of a nearby plant through, grinning broadly. Only long seconds after Viviette stood still beside the arbour did he swing his leg down.

'Oh, there you are.'

She wasn't sure what she wanted to do more – scream at him or break down crying. Somehow she did neither. On his other side Gideon turned towards her, squinting against the sunlight, and ran his eyes over her with a smirk that Jaghar would have punched off his face.

Jaghar...

'You asked for me,' she said stiffly, clutching her hands behind her back. 'But if I'm disturbing your little chat, I'll be happy to see you at any other moment.'

Or never at all, her thoughts added. She didn't speak them out loud.

'Bit touchy, isn't she?' Gideon said, shaking his head with a derisive grin lingering around his lips. Only then did he meet her eyes and nod a minimal bow. 'Good to see you again, Your Highness. You've grown into quite the beauty, haven't you?'

She wanted to gag. Not for your eyes. I'm younger than your daughters, in case you've forgotten. But again she didn't speak her mind – a lady had no business being clever, after all, and if she was unlucky, she would still need him in the future.

'Thank you, Lord Gideon.'

He ambled off, with a last amiable pat on Emeric's shoulder. Staying behind on the bench, basking in the golden morning light, her uncle was still grinning that self-satisfied grin – not the look of a man who'd lost a brother to a knife in the back mere days ago. Viviette swallowed her fury. She'd always known the relationship between him and her father was icy at best, but her father at least always made an effort to be pleasant on the superficial level. Emeric now abandoned even the appearances entirely.

'Well. Viviette. I haven't seen you much these days.'

'We rarely see each other much, Uncle.'

'Admittedly.' He chuckled. 'Have you been busy?'

'My father just died.'

'Yes, yes, but—'

'Could you get to the point?' Her composure was slipping from her grip like sand slipping through her fingers; five more minutes of pretending she was a polite, unaffected lady would probably leave her a sobbing mess on these charming, moss-covered cobblestones. 'You know well enough that we're – not dealing with this in the same way. I'd prefer just to hear why you wanted to speak with me.'

'Good gods, Viviette, calm down.' His voice had the undertone of the young men at Copper Coast who would make the most outrageous lewd comments while the chaperones were out of hearing, then indignantly claim they were obviously joking as soon as anyone told them to watch their words. 'I didn't want to burst into this all business-like, but if you insist...'

'I quite insist.'

'In that case.' He laid his fingertips against each other and tilted his head – nearly her father's gesture, and yet it looked different on him, a predator assessing where he could find her weak spots rather than a display of genuine curiosity. 'I heard you spoke with Reginald yesterday.'

Her throat tightened. Reginald. Seven stab wounds, in his own damned bed. Her clenched fist remembered the gold of her father's ring in her palm.

'So?'

'I'd like to hear what you spoke about.'

Viviette grabbed the first lie her mind presented to her – 'About a couple of letters he'd help me write. To

Emrys and Tamar, about what happened with Donovan and—'

'And that was all?'

'Yes? What else?'

He narrowed his eyes. 'Some rather different rumours are making the rounds.'

'There are always rumours making the rounds.'

'Rather persistent rumours. I've heard it alleged that Wymond is pushing the Council to ignore our inheritance laws. Laudine has apparently been going around this morning telling people that Trystan *wanted* to do so. According to her, that news came from Reginald. So allow me to wonder whether you're telling me the entire truth of that meeting yesterday.'

Viviette opened her mouth, sucked in a breath of strawberry-scented air, then paused. Sometimes, the work in the room of masks taught her, questions were the best answers.

'I don't fully understand why that would be of any importance to you?'

Now it was his turn to hesitate. Viviette tilted her head and waited. Of course she knew exactly why it mattered to him, and he knew she knew it, too – but he could hardly force her to admit that much. Which left him with two options: let it go and dismiss her without getting his answers, or admit that he simply wanted himself on that bloody throne...

He found a middle way.

'We have our inheritance laws for a reason, Viviette. I wouldn't want any chaos to ensue around the throne.'

'I'm not planning to cause chaos,' she said coolly. 'You can be assured I'll conform to the Council's decision, whatever it is.'

'And are you sure everyone will?' He made a wide gesture at the hall behind him. 'The Council meeting is public. If anyone hears of this nonsense and is unhappy with the outcome...'

'What do you want from me, then?'

He leaned back on his bench, breathing heavily. 'Did you ask Wymond to advocate for you?'

'Didn't need to.'

'That's not what I asked.'

'At the very least,' Viviette said curtly, 'I doubt he'd stop if I asked him to. He isn't doing anything he wouldn't be doing by himself. Anything else?'

'What did you discuss with Reginald?'

'Nothing of interest to you.'

'Gods be damned, Viviette!' His voice rose, as if he had forgotten they were still outside, and possibly within hearing distance of other inhabitants of the court. When had he last exchanged a serious word with her, she wondered with some bitter amusement – before Copper Coast? Had he expected she would apologetically crawl back to her room at his first request and beg the Council not to crown her? 'Are you in all seriousness entertaining the idea that they may put the silk cloak on *your* shoulders instead of—'

'Does that upset you?'

'You're a child! And an unmarried child at that! Nobody in his right mind would put a girl your age at the head of a kingdom!'

'Well,' Viviette said, forcing a smile. Her heart was a roaring fire. 'I think we can assume our Council nobles are generally in their right mind, so you shouldn't have much to worry about.'

He snorted. 'You seem to be well on your way to plant some solid nonsense in their mind, going by—'

'Does Wymond strike you as a man susceptible to nonsense?'

'I understand you're not going to give me a decent answer?'

'You seem to believe there is only one decent answer,' Viviette said coldly, 'and that is a passionate promise to stay out of your way and publicly demand that Wymond and Laudine vote for you at the Council meeting tomorrow. Which seems odd to me. The entire damned point of the Council is that they independently judge the candidates at these occasions – we are the last ones who should be influencing them, aren't we?'

'Then stop speaking to Wymond and—'

'Did you stop speaking to Gideon already?'

His hands tightened into fists. 'That's not—'

'No, of course that's not the same to you. Because you already decided they should crown you, didn't you?'

'As the laws dictate they should.'

'The laws dictate that whoever wins the Council should be crowned.' She tilted her head at him and frowned. 'And since when are you so passionate about being king, Uncle Emeric? I didn't hear you object when Father married me to Donovan, and that would decidedly have kept you off that throne as well.'

'Oh, for hell's sake.' He scoffed. 'Donovan would have needed a guardian for the Peaks while he was at the Floating Castle, remember? And you can be damn sure he'd have spent more time at home than in this godforsaken part of the world – I'd have been king in all but name for three quarters of the year. But of course you had to spoil all of it...'

"*I* spoiled it? How about *he* shouldn't have been holding his wife captive under his bedroom?'

'So what? Was she causing you trouble?'

Viviette stared at him, struggling for words. No, but he was a monster. No, but his bloody friends *would* have caused me trouble, and knowing the kind of men they are, you should realise exactly how bad it could have been.

'I'd rather die than marry a man like him.'

'Would you?' Something snake-like slid over his face as he stood up. 'In that case you'll have to hope I don't send you back to the Riverlands as soon as the Council crowns me, Viviette. Because Donovan is really causing quite a lot of trouble over you, do you realise that? For the wellbeing of the Peaks, it would definitely be much easier just to hand you over to him again.'

She barely dared to breathe. 'You wouldn't—'

'Better not to be too annoying, then,' he said, sauntering closer to her. Again she was reminded of a snake creeping up on her. 'Because I'll have to sacrifice the safety of the Peaks to keep you out of the Floating Castle, and of course, if you only spend your time undermining our stability anyway, it might—'

'Mind if I interrupt?' Jaghar's voice snapped behind her.

Viviette whirled around. He had appeared around the arbour with tangled blond hair and clenched fists, his mouth set in a hard line, his dark eyes shooting daggers at Emeric. Behind her, her uncle went unexpectedly quiet.

"*Jaghar*?'

'No objections?' he continued to Emeric, ignoring her. His raised eyebrow was a challenge, a hope for any excuse to draw a weapon. His fingers lay around the hilt of his knife with exactly the wrong stiffness about them. 'Good. I suggest you stay away from the princess for the days to come unless you want the Council to hear about this blatant attempt at blackmail. As a matter of fact, I suggest you stay away from any Council members in general, unless you'd like certain rumours to stick up their head in the hours to come. Clear?'

'Who do you think you—'

'Someone with information you wouldn't like to spread. Are you leaving?'

'What do you mean, information I—'

'Let's put it this way,' Jaghar said, too slowly, his upper lip curling up in a gesture as if to bite him. 'If you're not out of here *very* damned quickly, if you're not making *very* sure to stay out of the princess's way from now on, I might well find myself planting a knife between *your* treasonous shoulder blades one of these days. Need me to elaborate?'

Viviette stared at him, the ground sinking away beneath her feat. The bewildered shadows in his eyes, the way his fingers still tensed around his knife hilt. Emeric's treasonous shoulder blades. No. No, he couldn't be saying what she thought he was saying. But her uncle paled, and the sudden alarm in his expression suggested he knew exactly what they were speaking about...

Emeric?

Emeric?

He strode forward so abruptly that she jolted back; she only barely managed to suppress a shriek. Beside her, Jaghar didn't yield an inch.

'Pity.' His voice was a low growl. 'Was hoping you'd give me an excuse.'

'I have no idea what madness you're drivelling about, Androughan,' Emeric snapped, forcing an icy chuckle. 'But you should know better than throwing out such unholy accusations at a man who'll be your king in a day.'

He stalked off without waiting for an answer, leaving the two of them alone in a sun-drenched silence that no longer seemed so warm and light at all.

CHAPTER 10

Jaghar pulled his fingers off his knife and sucked in a lungful of fresh air in some useless attempt to calm himself. He might as well have inhaled a roaring fire. His heartbeat didn't slow down in the slightest, the rage burning in his chest refused to fade. He shouldn't have been so reckless, he knew. He shouldn't have been so forthright about all he knew – but demon be damned, to find the bastard anywhere near *Velvet* after this night from hell...

'Jaghar?'

That one word contained a hundred questions, and just as many suspicions. She stood staring at him in the golden sunlight, her black dress too dark for her pale face, her thoughts visibly whirring behind her green eyes. Somehow she looked – strangely unchanged. The whole world looked unfathomably unaltered, as a matter of fact, with its roses and its sunlight and its pleasant summer breeze – as if none of last night had ever happened. As if Reginald had never even died. As if he hadn't just promised his hand to another woman mere hours ago, and found out he *had* kindly opened the door for Trystan's murderer after all...

He felt stained. Contaminated. A sticky, greasy feeling lingering just below his skin, a darkness tagging along at his every step; part of him was surprised the leaves and flowers didn't wither to dust around him.

And then there was Velvet.

Staring at him with so much honest concern, so much trust, that he wanted to curl up to a little ball on the cobblestones and cry his heart out until the world had somehow fixed itself around him – until he could forget about Rosin, could forget about what he had done. Couldn't she at the very least look a little more annoyed at his disappearance of last night? Show a little more justified anger at his overhurried entrance? At least then he wouldn't feel so ashamed to even be looking at her, frightened and beautiful, her slender shoulders tense as if she already knew what he might be about to tell her...

Hell's sake. He barely knew what he was about to tell her himself.

'Morning,' he managed. The word felt jarringly normal on his lips. Morning. As if this was just another day, just another garden walk. 'Are you...'

'Hell's sake – *Jaghar*.'

She flew into his arms with so much force he nearly stumbled backwards, and clutched her arms around him with a smothered, sob-like sound. He stiffened at the touch. Garden, his thoughts screamed. People. Danger. Then the scent of her perfume found him, and his mind split in two at the first whiff of that flowery fragrance – one half that wanted to hold her for the rest of this day, damn the watching eyes and the whispers, and then a half that remembered the dark hours he had spent sitting cold and paralysed at the edge of the abyss last night, unable to think, unable to move... He couldn't stop to hold her now. He had finally made his plans, worked out his timing. If he paused, he would never get going again.

'Velvet...'

'Don't you dare to ever do that again,' she muttered into his shirt, holding him so tightly he had trouble breathing. 'Running out like that – disappearing like that. Next time I'll damn well come after you if you don't give me a proper explanation first, Spymaster – I was afraid – I nearly thought...'

Her sentence died away into nothingness, fears too unspeakable to bring them over her lips. Jaghar swallowed down the bile rising in his throat and wrapped his arms around her, feeling like he was somehow sullying her, tainting the softness of her skin. But she didn't let go of him, and he didn't have the strength to pull away.

'I'm sorry,' he whispered. Words so hopelessly inadequate it was nearly laughable. 'I'm so sorry, I didn't want you to worry – I...' He swallowed again. I almost killed your father. Your father died because of me. 'I wasn't in any – any decent state of mind, if that's anything...'

She looked up. Too gentle, too concerned. 'Oh, good gods, Jaghar – what happened?'

'Emeric,' he managed. The easy part. She wouldn't blame him for her uncle's treason. 'Emeric killed...'

'Oh, gods.'

'I'm so sorry.' How often would he repeat those words today? 'I wish I could make it untrue, but...'

'But how's that *possible*,' she said, interrupting him with a clear, sharp voice, hardly a trace of the shock left in her words. Her hands tensed in his lower back. 'I thought Madelena checked his movements – wasn't he one of the people who didn't leave their room at all that evening? Did he hire someone else to do it?'

Jaghar shook his head, the knowledge burning on his tongue. He knew what he had to do now – not just Emeric, he had to say. It was Rosin, too – the woman I showed around in this castle, the woman I forgot to keep an eye on even though I knew she wasn't done with me yet. The woman who wants me to marry her. And then she would be furious – then she'd *have* to be furious, and he'd apologise until he had no words left to speak, and it might still not be enough.

But when he opened his mouth, no word came out.

'Jaghar?'

146

How could the trees still rustle so calmly around them
– how did the sun still manage to shine so bright? He
had to speak. He had to explain himself. But his words
were running aground like a ship in shallow water, and
every next breath, every next attempt only dug them in
deeper.

'Jaghar, what's the matter?'

'I'm sorry,' he whispered, closing his eyes. Cold, dark
disgust washed over him. 'Can I just say – I'm sorry – if
you're angry at me I promise I understand, I promise...'

'What in the world *happened*?' Her voice turned
sharper. 'Are you—'

A loud, high-pitched giggle tore through the silence
behind his back.

Velvet jumped away from him, her eyes shooting
around with sudden panic. Only then did Jaghar hear
the footsteps approaching behind the rose-covered
arbour, the whispering voices and muffled chortles
he had missed through the blur in his head. Two or
three young women, making little attempt to hide their
approach.

Oh, demon be damned. Every single person in the
garden had seen Emeric stalk off. Of course they were
coming to take a look.

'Jaghar!' Velvet whispered. 'Jaghar, please – they'll
think – they'll know...'

It took a physical effort to straighten his shoulders
and draw his most lifeless expression over his face. Her
green eyes clung to his face even with her entire body
leaning away from him, her look a mixture of panic

and incomprehension. For a heartbeat he was sure, frighteningly sure that whoever would step into view the next moment would find them like that, drowning in each other's eyes despite the superficial distance between them – and worse, for a heartbeat he could barely care.

Then Velvet closed her eyes and said, loud enough for the approaching ladies to hear, 'Thank you, Spymaster, I'm doing well enough. But it is kind of you to keep me informed of your progress. I suppose you don't mind if I return to my room now?'

Once he had enjoyed it, this game they were playing – the excitement of their shared secrets, her skilful acting, green eyes cooling down whenever anyone came too close to their conversations. Most of all, her body melting to his as soon as the world left them alone again. But he didn't want to play games anymore. Gods be damned, he just wanted to love her for the world to see.

But their audience was coming closer, and he couldn't afford to be honest now.

'Not at all,' he said, taking care to keep his voice cold and flat, the voice the court knew from him. Not the voice he wanted her to hear from him now, for hell's sake. Her eyes darted over his shoulder for the shortest moment; he supposed the giggling ladies had finally stepped into view. At least her smile turned even more bland in the same moment.

'Wonderful.' She nodded at him, then hesitated and added, 'And please don't mind my uncle too much. He's always been quite uncontrolled when he's emotional. Your news must have hit him a little unpleasantly.'

With his back towards their audience, he dared to allow a quick smile, even if he didn't feel it, even if he'd scream rather than smile. Giving the world an explanation for Emeric's dramatic exit that not only put all blame on her uncle, but subtly portrayed him as an unstable candidate for the throne as well – quite an achievement within a few short sentences.

'Thank you, Princess.' He stepped aside. 'I won't keep you up for longer, then.'

'Much appreciated, Spymaster.'

Somehow he managed not to grab her arm and pull her against him as she passed him by on her way back inside. A few minutes. As soon as she was out of sight, as soon as it was clear to the court that he wasn't following her, he could make his way to her room through the hidden corridors and finally explain the full story to her...

His guts cramped up. And then? Then she might be devastated. She might be furious. She might blame him for the entire mess, or she might not do any such thing at all.

Regardless, then he'd have to deal with Emeric.

No time to lose. In little less than an hour he'd have to meet with Rosin again – another thought that made his intestines twist in unpleasant ways. By now Velvet should at least be inside, and even the ladies furiously whispering behind him couldn't accuse him of following her.

Yet when he stepped around the arbour, back into view for the rest of the garden, he found her barely fifteen feet away from him, stopped in her tracks by the stiff-shouldered, thin-lipped mass of black lace and silver hair that was Lady Laudine of Greyside. As he approached the two women, careful not to meet Velvet's gaze, he just heard the duchess finish her sentence, in the strict tone of an old governess.

'... hope you have time for a cup of tea and a short conversation?'

He did look up, then, before he could help himself. A glimpse of green, then Velvet had averted her eyes again – but that short shared look told him enough about the thoughts flashing through her mind. After Wymond, Laudine was the best ally they had. There was no sense in slighting her, and she *would* be slighted if Velvet gave the impression she had anything more important on her mind than the young man Laudine had found murdered in his own bed the previous night.

For hell's sake – couldn't the world leave them alone for a *minute* on this morning from hell?

'Of course!' Velvet said as he passed her by. The perfect polite young lady, exactly the humble, well-mannered princess that Laudine would want to see. 'I was already hoping I would find you around the castle this morning, my lady – the Spymaster informed me about Reginald just a moment ago, I still have trouble wrapping my head around it...'

Just what she should have said. Jaghar knew she had no other option. And yet it took all he had not to turn back around, wrap his arms around her and drag her inside, away from the watching eyes and the curious whispers. Damn Reginald, and damn that cup of tea. He needed her now – couldn't the rest of the world at least understand that much?

He restrained himself, though. A princess who started illicit affairs with her own father's Spymaster was likely not a princess Laudine would ever vote for.

He waited in her bedroom for half an hour, pacing from the window to the hearth and back to the window so many times that he nearly expected his feet to leave permanent furrows in the granite floor. Outside the sun climbed higher and higher into the stark blue summer sky. Velvet did not show up. How long could Laudine need to make the point that her nephew shouldn't have died, and that Emeric should never end up with a crown on his head?

Jaghar muttered a curse. Longer than half an hour, it turned out.

He sank into the chair at her desk and pulled a sheet of scrap parchment from the upper drawer. If she didn't return before he had to go see Rosin, at the very least he could give her an explanation for his absence, some answers to her questions.

Velvet, he scrabbled down. Then he stared at the parchment, a nagging headache emerging behind his eyes.

What was he supposed to write next? Sorry I couldn't stay around, I'm off to go see the woman who killed your father for me. Love you. Jaghar. Demon be damned, that wasn't the kind of revelation you could put in a letter, was it? Emeric's treason alone would have been bearable, perhaps, but this was far more than Emeric's treason – this was Rosin's viciousness, and worse...

His thoughts wavered. Worse, his own stupidity. Rosin had made clear enough she wouldn't let go of him, in that last conversation before he had followed Velvet to the Riverlands – and yet he had not even thought of keeping an eye on her at their return to Rock Hall. Velvet could hardly overlook how miserably he had failed her, if not worse, and did he really want her to come to that realisation alone, with no idea when he'd even be back?

With another curse he dipped her pen in the ink again. *Hope Laudine didn't give you too much trouble. I need to go see some people to get our evidence against Emeric.* At least he wouldn't run out without an explanation this time. *If you wait for me here, I'll be back as soon as possible to explain the full story. Couple of hours at most.*

He hesitated a last moment, then added, quickly, *Love you*. Most of the servants couldn't read anyway, and he didn't expect anyone else would come in to snoop.

Still not a brilliant letter – as a matter of fact, she might still be rather unhappy about the lack of answers it contained – but he couldn't think of anything that *would* make her happy with the current state of affairs...

And he didn't have time to linger. With a curse he folded the letter before he could waste another five minutes hesitating, and left it on her desk as he hurried out of the room, out of Rock Hall. Less than half an hour, and he'd have to be in town to meet with Rosin – a meeting he couldn't delay, no matter how badly he wanted to delay it. There was too much risk to the plans he had made in the cold light of the rising sun that morning, too much she could mess up if she wanted to; he needed all the time he could get to smooth out whatever trouble she might cause. Because he had to be done with her in time. Her role had to be over and done as soon as possible. If he still needed her to save Velvet's crown tomorrow morning, by the time he had promised her a marriage...

That couldn't happen. That couldn't, *couldn't* happen.

CHAPTER 11

V iviette stared at the parchment trembling in her hands, too stupefied to even curse.

I need to go see some people. Fine, she could imagine that much. Laudine had taken her time – it had taken a long hour of unnervingly polite conversation before the old duchess finally seemed satisfied with their shared opinions on Reginald's death, Emeric's character and Peak politics in general. If Jaghar had made his own appointments last night, it made sense he couldn't make them wait. *Evidence against Emeric.* She could hardly object to that point either. But then there was the last part of his short message.

If you wait for me here, I'll be back as soon as possible to explain the full story.

Which did not make any sense at all.

If he had been writing anyway, he could just as well have included that explanation too. Surely he didn't expect her to suddenly collapse at the revelation of whatever devious plan her uncle had made to get into her father's study unnoticed? Or was the full story so complex that he couldn't possibly write it down in the time he had spent waiting for her? That didn't sound very likely either – at the very least he could have *tried*.

She threw herself back onto her bed and stared at the dark grey ceiling without blinking, her thoughts sweeping slow, careful rounds through her head. Something was wrong, she felt it in the depth of her bones. Something was terribly wrong. If the explanation was a simple story of Emeric avoiding the watching eyes of Jaghar's people...

A stab of scorching hate burned through her at the thought of her uncle. Damn the bastard – damn him a thousand times. Where was he now, pompous and pleased with himself, without the tiniest shred of regret at the knife he had stabbed into his own brother's back? No wonder he had been so alarmed when he heard the rumours of Wymond pulling votes to her side. No wonder, too, that Jaghar had insisted she'd be well-protected even in her own room.

She glanced at the door, unable to suppress a shiver. Emeric had to know she knew, or at least suspected him, after that scene in the garden. But at least he'd have trouble passing the two square-shouldered men at her door, even if Jaghar was nowhere around.

Jaghar. She fell back into her pillows and closed her eyes.

It couldn't just be Emeric. If this was just a matter of her uncle sneaking into her father's study and – hell's sake, *killing* him – she couldn't explain why Jaghar had looked so utterly aghast this morning. Why he had insisted on apologising a dozen times before even telling her anything. Why he hadn't just written down what he'd discovered. And there *had* to be more going on, because someone should have seen Emeric if he had simply walked to that study indeed…

Keep a look on everything around her. Secret doors, too

The corridors.

Had Emeric used the *corridors*?

But how was that possible? He shouldn't know about them. Even her father hadn't known about them until Jaghar had discovered the secret again, and she doubted either of them had ever trusted Emeric with the knowledge. So who else could have told her uncle?

Some member of the service?

A traitor among his own people would at least give Jaghar a damn good reason to look like the world had been pulled out from under his feet tonight. But then why wouldn't he just sit down with her and discuss strategies and plans, rather than storm out with only half of an explanation to go make some undefined arrangements with undefined people in undefined places? For some reason the arrangements, or the people, or the places had to be a problem.

The question was, then, whether it was a *good* reason.

Viviette muttered a curse at nobody in particular. What would be a good reason? Was anyone threatening to slit her throat if he told her more? But she had never seen him cave to physical threats, and even if he was scared for her safety – wouldn't he come up with some clever way to get her out of danger?

A sliver of doubt wormed through her. Did he believe he ought to protect her from some unpleasant truth, some detail her sensitive stomach wasn't able to handle? The poor little princess again, who should be protected by everything and everyone around her...

She sat up again, suppressing a next curse. No, that was nonsense. She knew better. He'd seen her solve murders and be an accomplice to them, too. He had told her she wasn't weak. Whatever was going on, this couldn't be it.

But then what in the world was the problem?

'I damn well hope you'll come back with a decent explanation, Spymaster,' she muttered to the tapestry hiding the secret door to her room. Quite to her disappointment, he didn't step out at once to apologise and give the full report of his night and morning.

Well.

What now?

I'll be back, the letter said. A couple of hours at most.

A couple of *hours*.

Only now did the frustration swell in her, delayed by the shock of the situation. He wanted her to wait in her room for *hours*? While he was gods-knew-where, arranging his mysterious businesses with his mysterious people, solving a murder that was becoming a bloody family affair to her? While the Council would meet in less than twenty-four hours to determine the fate of her kingdom?

She jumped up, her limbs buzzing with restlessness. Good reasons or not, she had better things to do than waiting. Even if she had to stay away from Emeric, there were still some Council votes to be won – at least Eluard's pleasant smiles suggested he wasn't vehemently opposed to voting in her favour, and she had no idea at all what the newly arrived Gerald thought of the matter. She might as well try to steer them in the right direction a little.

She was already making for the door before her conscious mind caught up with the plan. If Jaghar wasn't around, she needed someone else for the necessary information. Where could Madelena be around this time of the day?

It took no more than a few quick questions to one of the men still guarding her bedroom door; within fifteen minutes the plucky, red-haired girl who went by the name of Branwen hurried up to her to whisper that Madelena would be at her office as soon as possible. Indeed Jaghar's right hand came strolling into the corridor moments after Viviette arrived herself, with a quick nod at the men still standing around in the shadows and a simple 'Morning, Your Highness.'

Viviette quietly waited until the other woman found her keys and held the door for her; she slipped into the small room with a feeling of both excitement and dread, the piles of spies' notes mingling with the memory of two nights ago, the hours she had spent in numb shock until Jaghar returned from his first examinations. The pain rose to nowhere the same heights now, as though her body itself had pushed the grief aside to wait for a more opportune moment.

'So,' Madelena said, closing the door behind her, her voice all calm and reason. 'Did you get any sleep last night?'

'A little,' Viviette said, with a wry attempt at a smile. A few nightmarish shreds. Hours of tossing and turning in the dark, mostly. 'Have you seen him this morning? Or did he only storm in to tell Emeric off and run out again?'

Madelena raised an eyebrow and sat down in the chair behind the desk. 'Haven't seen a trace of him. What's the matter with Emeric?'

'Killed my father, apparently.'

Madelena froze. 'That's – quite impossible. Are you sure—'

'I said the same thing, but Laudine pulled me away before he could tell me more. Based on what he said yesterday...' She hesitated. 'Could he have used the corridors?'

'Emeric shouldn't know about the corridors.'

'Are you very sure? No chance that any of your people told him about them?'

'I damn well hope they didn't,' Madelena said dryly. 'He's not popular with us, at least, and even if he were...'

'You wouldn't expect spies to go blathering around about their knowledge.'

'Exactly.'

Viviette took a seat as well, the anxiety still rummaging through her veins. 'No other ideas either?'

'Not the faintest. Are you sure he was sure about...'

'Yes.'

'Well,' Madelena said, with an unfazed nod. 'I can send some people after it?'

'I'm a bit reluctant to do much around Emeric,' Viviette said quickly. 'Jaghar said he's trying to get his hands on some evidence, and I don't want to interfere with – well, whatever plan he may have.'

Madelena sighed. 'I see. Fair point.'

'So I was wondering if you had any news on the Council.'

'Ah.' A seemingly random page of notes was pulled from the middle of a pile, without a trace of hesitation. Running her eyes over the scribbles of ink, Madelena said, 'Osric and Gideon vote for Emeric. Laudine seems to have been pretty happy with you, based on her remarks to Wymond that Branwen just told me about...'

Viviette's heart made a little jump.

'... and then we have Aldred, Gerald and Eluard, whose preferences are unclear so far. Although Aldred is of course the one who sent his own nephew to the gallows for murdering a man who was harassing his wife, because it was technically unlawful. He might be uninclined to vote in Emeric's favour if Jaghar manages to get any evidence.'

Viviette closed her eyes. Hope and frustration were competing for preference in her chest. If Jaghar managed to persuade the Council's oldest and most respected member, that was enough to immediately forget about this long morning without information – and yet, why couldn't he *tell* her... And what in the world was he doing now? Was he at the very least safe?

A couple of hours. She'd have to keep herself busy until he was back to explain the situation.

'Anything on Gerald and Eluard?' she said.

'Very little. Gerald arrived in the early morning. I invited him...' Quite against her habits, Madelena hesitated.

'To the room of masks?' Viviette finished.

'You know about the room?'

Despite everything, she nearly smiled. 'I've heard a thing or two about it, yes.'

'Good gods. You know about – Jaghar's work there, too?'

'Yes, of course.'

Madelena opened her mouth, then leaned back in her chair and folded her arms. 'With all due respect, Your Highness, I'm starting to wonder who of you two is more insane.'

'Pretty sure it's me,' Viviette said. 'So, about Gerald – he was interested?'

'Of course.' A snort. 'His type always is. Young and stupid and too cowardly to ever speak a word with a woman he isn't paying. I'll send someone to his room tonight, will let you know if he has anything interesting to say.'

'Thanks – and Eluard?'

'I had Paulette invite him to the service after he arrived tonight. Wasn't interested.'

'Alright,' Viviette said slowly. Two targets, then. If she could get a single one of them to her side – and if Jaghar managed to convince Aldred that Emeric quite clearly violated the law...

'Plans?' Madelena interrupted her thoughts.

'Oh, nothing in particular.' That was at least partly a lie. She didn't have *plans*, admittedly, not in the clear-cut, tightly scheduled way that Jaghar seemed to have planned whatever in hell he was doing – but ideas were definitely bubbling up. Most of them decidedly unwise, and yet...

She had to do *something*, didn't she?

'I'll see what I come up with,' she added. 'Perhaps I get something out of them. What rooms did they get?'

Madelena gave her a rather sceptical look. 'With all due respect again, but do you have any experience with these things?'

'A little,' Viviette said modestly.

'How little, exactly?'

'Remember when we suddenly knew that Mauno planned to get unpleasant if he didn't get his way?'

Madelena's eyebrows came up so slowly that Viviette barely saw them moving. 'Mauno.'

'Yes.'

'I mostly remember that Jaghar was looking quite unpleasant about him. More than about any other person in the world, that is.'

Quite unpleasant. About the man who had ruined his life and then happily tried to ruin it a second time.

'I think I best not say too much about that, really.'

'You do know more?'

'I do get things out of people, usually.'

Madelena gave her a long, taxing look. Only after a silence that seemed to last hours did she sit up and say, 'Gerald is staying in the third room on the second floor, Eluard has the room left to Wymond's. Let me know if you hear anything interesting.'

'Will do.'

'And if you manage to find out what in the world Jaghar is doing...'

'Yes,' Viviette said, averting her eyes. A couple of hours. *I'll be back.* Where *was* he? 'I'll let you know.'

Her vague outline had grown into a full-fledged plan by the time she reached her room and locked out her guardians again.

It wasn't a wise plan by any means – reckless was the best she could say about it, and ridiculous might be a more accurate description. She could be recognised.

She could run into a few spies too many at the wrong moments. Madelena might figure out where Kara from Copper Coast had disappeared to. And even if that miraculously would happen, she'd have to stand the hands on her –

She shivered. Now pull yourself together, Velvet. Someone needs to do it.

She checked her bedroom lock one more time and let down her hair. It took some digging to find her familiar peignoir in the back of her closet; she hadn't used it since her father announced her engagement to Donovan. For a moment she barely managed to move, the memory tearing at her heart in all the wrong ways – to think that he had honestly believed he was doing her a favour, with all that happened since...

With a brusque shrug she shoved that thought aside, burying it underneath the pile of plans and obligations – not now. She couldn't afford to grieve. There would be time to collapse later; now she first had to take care of what needed to be done.

Gerald.

Eluard.

And the first would doubtlessly be easiest.

She felt strangely naked, finding her way to the room of masks without the protection of her own velvet mask on her face – she had no idea where it had gone after she left it in Jaghar's room on the morning before her departure to the Higher Riverlands. But nobody else was roaming the corridors around this time, not even Emeric, and she found the room deserted. The first few chests were filled with clothes ranging from lacy nightgowns to chaste Temple dresses and an arsenal of accessories that nearly made her blush. The fourth one contained a collection of unused masks. She picked a dark blue one, sewn from smooth silk – it seemed appropriate to today's fight.

Routine crept onto her as she made her way towards the guest tower. This was business as usual again, business as it had been before she left Rock Hall for Donovan – the exhilarating thrill of being someone else entirely, of pretending to be nothing but a body and setting her mind to work instead...

Except she hadn't even thought about touching anyone else again after Jaghar had asked her to marry him on that idyllic lakeside in Redwood.

Then again, she hadn't expected him to start acting like the secretive Spymaster from her youth, either.

Her heart shrunk a little, frustration and concern in equal amounts. What in the world was he *doing*? But there was no sense in thinking about that now – he'd probably have an explanation for his disappearance of the past hours, and either way, she had a Council to win first.

She waited a few minutes for the castle's normal corridors to go empty. Then she slipped out of the hidden doorway and knocked on the door of the third room. It took only a few seconds for Gerald to open.

The duke stared at her with obvious surprise for a few heartbeats, his high forehead wrinkled in a frown that made him look even younger and even less intelligent.

Then he grinned, an expression that looked strangely aggressive despite his weak chin.

'I honestly thought it was all some joke.'

'Sorry to disappoint, my lord,' she said, her melodious Copper Coast accent twice as thick just to be sure he wouldn't accidentally recognise her voice tomorrow morning. 'Would you like to let me in?'

He stepped aside, still grinning, closed the door behind her and said, 'I thought you'd be here only in the evening?'

'That's normal procedure, yes.' Viviette smiled a teasing smile at him. 'But of course with new clients, we like to... get to know them a little. So in case there's anything I can help with?'

'Anything you...' His grin grew broader, his eyes running over her body in the most shamelessly obvious way. Then, abruptly, he stepped back. 'One question – er – I take it this is all treated – well, fully confidential? I wouldn't want – well – you understand.'

Viviette tilted her head. 'Do you have a wife, my lord?'

'Oh, no – not yet, I'd say—'

'Ah, an engagement, then?'

'Of sorts.' An awkward grin. 'Her father still needs to give permission, but I'm hopeful that won't be a problem after this week.'

'Oh?' Viviette said, inviting herself to sit down in the nearest chair and planting her chin on her fist in her most interested posture, her peignoir falling open in what was not an invitation yet, but definitely a promise. 'Anything spectacular on the planning this week?'

Gerald threw a glance at the closed door, then turned back to her and lowered his voice. 'You can keep a secret, can't you?'

'That's half of my job, my lord.'

He chuckled uncomfortably. 'Of course, of course – look, don't tell anyone, but Athelina happens to be the daughter of a – well, colleague of mine.'

Athelina? Viviette nearly jolted up. Good gods – Aldred's daughter. 'Oh, is she?'

'So I'll have a word with him one of these days,' Gerald continued, looking unbearably smug. 'Old man will see that we agree on all the important matters in life. No doubt he'll be happy to wed his daughter to me once he knows we're of one mind when it comes to politics and law and all of that – yes, I've got it all planned.' He winked at her. 'But of course, until I'm officially an engaged man...'

'Ah, yes,' Viviette said, and managed to drag something like a smile from between her spinning thoughts – *one mind when it comes to politics and law.* The spineless bastard was just going to vote whatever Aldred voted, wasn't he? Gods be damned. 'Well, we'll make sure to be discreet, then. Any other particulars to keep in mind?'

'Eh – not that I—'

'Absolutely wonderful.' She stood up and took a step back in the same movement, away from him, towards the door. Damn the fool, with his non-existent chin and his hungry eyes. She knew what she needed to know. Madelena could smooth out the rest, for all she cared.

'Well, in that case, make sure to be in your room tonight and...'

'Are you leaving?' His confusion was obvious, and with the silk peignoir clinging to her hips, she could hardly blame him. She gave him her most confident smile nonetheless.

'See you later, my lord.'

And she was out, away from his greedy looks, striding past a shocked servant girl who didn't look like she'd be very discreet about lord Gerald's visitors at all.

CHAPTER 12

'Just to be clear,' Jaghar hissed, turning around in the dusky corridor. 'If you mess any of this up, you're dead. No clever plans. No clever warnings to Emeric or anyone else. No...'

'Don't *worry* so much, Jaghar.' Rosin seemed genuinely indignant as she shook her red curls over her shoulder, a gesture he knew too well, and that made him itch to drag her out of the castle by her hair today. Don't worry so much. After she killed the man who'd been his sole reason to live for years. After the agony of the past night, the dark, nauseating guilt still burning in him... *Don't worry.*

'Wouldn't have lived to this age without worrying,' he snapped, and she clucked her tongue behind him, as though he were a little boy saying something endearingly silly. Again he nearly drew his knife at the sound alone. One more hour, he told himself for what might be the hundredth time – if it all went according to plan, if she'd do her job one more time, then the evidence would be out, and he would finally have the time to confess his sins to Velvet and hope she'd somehow make sense of the world again...

One more hour, and Rosin's help wouldn't be a necessity to him anymore.

They finally reached the end of the corridor – her presence behind him alone made a walk of minutes feel like an exhausting hike. As he opened the door to the room behind, Jaghar gestured her to stay in her place. She obeyed with a quiet snort.

Inside the room – empty since the king's aunt died five years ago – he found Vander, his dust rag still in his hand. More than a sharp 'And?' wasn't needed.

'More or less on schedule.' Vander coughed. 'One unexpected circumstance – Branwen told Aldred that Emeric wanted to speak with him about the Council meeting, but was overheard by Eluard. Who promptly announced he'd like to come as well.'

Jaghar raised an eyebrow. 'How so?'

'Has been talking with Wymond. I think he suspects Emeric is trying to push the Council to his side – everybody knows Aldred is supposed to be an influential vote. Anyway, Aldred was of the opinion that

Emeric couldn't have anything private to say, legally speaking.'

'So they're both coming.'

'Looks like it.'

Jaghar considered that for half a second, then decided it wasn't worth the hassle to discourage Eluard. It might even be helpful to have another critical ear around. He had picked Aldred as his witness because the old man would never tell a lie, and just as important, because nobody would have the guts to accuse him of lying either – but if Eluard was indeed open to Wymond's line of argumentation...

'Fine. So how long do we have?'

'About five minutes, I'd say.'

'Good.' He glanced at the direction of Emeric's room, three doors away. 'You wait here for my sign. Will see you in minutes.'

Vander nodded, fidgeting with his rag. Jaghar stepped back into the corridor, where Rosin stood leaning against the walls with her arms folded and her smile still as triumphant as it had been all morning.

'Pretty clever, Jaghar.'

'Shut your mouth and come with me.'

She giggled as she followed him to the nearest door leading to the castle's open corridors. His blood was rushing in his ears – an hour, he repeated to himself, an hour at most and she'd no longer be a necessity to him – an hour at most and justice could finally be done...

An hour at most, and he'd see Velvet again.

'You still remember everything?' he hissed, turning around at the doorway. She rolled her eyes.

'I haven't suddenly turned stupid, Jaghar. I go to his room. I leave the door on a chink. I ask my questions. He talks. I leave, you marry me.'

His fists were itching. 'Right. Better be off, then.'

She smiled another elated smile at him as she passed him and slipped out into the unconcealed part of the castle. Jaghar had to take three quick breaths to calm down his heart and convince himself not to drag her back and slam her head against the wall a couple of times – *you marry me*. A side note on the list, the self-evident conclusion to a plan she had been brooding on for far too long. For a moment the doubt got a hold of him. She hadn't suddenly turned stupid indeed – she should know her role would be over as soon as she left Emeric's room. And yet she went along with his plan uncannily easily... Had he missed anything?

But that wasn't a question for this moment. He kicked himself back into motion and hurried to the room where Vander was waiting for him – not a minute to lose, now.

'Ready?' Vander said as soon as he appeared again. He sounded tense.

'Yes. Ready. Off you go.'

His spy slipped out of the room, leaving this door on a chink as well. Jaghar positioned himself just around the doorway, invisible for those passing by outside, and closed his eyes. Now the timing had to be perfect. No second chances, no room for mistakes. Rosin knew, and if she wanted to, she was skilled enough to get it done. But that was assuming she wanted to get it done at once – assuming she'd allow him to be done with her so easily...

Several times footsteps approached, and several times he jolted up only to be disappointed. Then, finally, Vander's voice again, in a harrowed whisper of which he could barely make out the words as they passed his half-open door –

'I'm so sorry to disturb you like this, my lords, but I couldn't walk away without you hearing – it's that room. I think we should be quiet now...'

A muttered confirmation in what sounded like Eluard's voice, then silence. Jaghar slipped into the secret corridor again and quietly opened the hidden door to Emeric's room – the door about which the bastard knew since he had used it to kill his own bloody brother through it.

'... but how did you manage that part?'

Rosin's voice reached him in its most infuriating tone, that teasing, superficial lightness she had so successfully used to convince him for years that he didn't actually hate her... He clenched his fists to keep quiet. 'Did he even know you were there? Or did you just step in and – like *that* – kill him?'

Jaghar couldn't see her gesture at the *that* through the tapestry covering the open door. Even without visual signs, he knew she sounded too gleeful about it.

By now, he assumed, Vander and his dukes had reached the other door to Emeric's room as well. The door that Rosin should have left ajar, if all was well.

'He never even noticed me,' Emeric said, and he, too, sounded cheerful, as if recounting the story of a happy summer's day picnic. 'I opened that door you showed me – as quietly as you said it would be – and he was sitting with his back towards me, reading some boring report. All I had to do—'

'No, no, tell me more! So you opened that door – he was alone, wasn't he? Did you make sure he was alone at first?'

Hell be damned, she *was* good. He had allowed himself to forget it the past months, all too happy to believe she was forever a thing of the past – had wondered at times why in the world he kept her in his service for so long. This had to be at least part of the answer – how effortlessly she strung the conversation along, how easy she made it for Emeric to spill every detail of his guilt to her.

'Yes, yes, of course I did – I'm not an idiot.' Emeric laughed his most pedantic laugh, and Jaghar was overcome, for a single blood-curdling moment, by an urge to jump up, tear the tapestry aside, and kill the bastard here and now. 'I knew he'd be seeing the Androughan, wasn't going to walk into the room with that dog around to protect him – but after dinner I saw he was busy running after my niece...'

'Oh, was he?' Rosin's voice was pure poison now. 'Silly of him, you'd say.'

Jaghar pressed his nails into his hand palms until the pain was sharp enough to sting through the red-hot haze in his mind – silly of him. Damn you, Rosin. You know I'd have given my life to protect him. You know I lay awake at night regretting my own carelessness. You know I'll understand you're speaking to me now, not to him –

But Emeric laughed, oblivious of the ears listening along with every word.

'Never understood why the fool wanted to keep some foreign savage around in the first place – told him from the beginning it would cause him nothing but trouble. Anyway, I checked if his study was empty, then walked in, found him working and just... did it.'

'You stabbed him.'

'I damn well stabbed him.' Another laugh that sent boiling fury up Jaghar's veins. 'Serves him right, after all those years – I knew we were never too fond of each other, but to blatantly pass me by for some girl who can't even keep a husband interested?'

'Unheard of, really.'

'Can hardly bear to think – if you hadn't warned me...'

'Oh, you're *very* welcome,' Rosin said, in her most coquettish voice, and again Jaghar knew she wasn't speaking to Emeric anymore. 'So tell me more – how did it *feel*? You must have felt a *little* bit of hesitation, no?'

Jaghar turned around and strode off, clenching his jaws so tightly it hurt. How did it feel to murder your own brother with a knife in the back? He didn't want to know. He didn't want or need to imagine it any more vividly than he already did – Emeric sneaking up on that quiet figure at the desk, the knife swinging down, the sound –

He gagged. Behind him, Rosin's dazzling laugh followed him through the corridor. Not meant for Emeric. He had never heard her laugh like that at any of their clients. She wasn't staging this little theatre for Trystan's brother himself anymore, or even for the dukes listening along outside the door – this was for him, a punishment for leaving her, a warning of all the ways she wouldn't hesitate to hurt him if he ever dared to do the same again. He shut the door behind him without the tiniest hint of relief, her voice still in his head – *silly of him, you'd say...*

And she wasn't even wrong.

Oh, Velvet. Who made it so easy, after all those years, to see how Rosin played him, used his fear of being a monster against him until he believed she was the best he deserved – and here he was, failing her, betraying her, while Rosin once again set off every painful weapon in her arsenal.

Shivers ran through him, the sleepless night and the fear finally catching up with him as he sat there with his back against the cold stone and breathed the dusty smell of this unused bedroom. He couldn't marry her. He *couldn't* marry her. Even if Velvet didn't want him anymore, even if she'd throw him out of the castle as soon as she heard the story of her father's death, he'd rather end up at the bottom of the abyss than tied to Rosin in any way. A few more minutes and she'd be done, he tried to convince himself, but with the sharp hooks of her voice still fixed in his mind, it suddenly seemed ridiculously optimistic to believe she'd allow him to do away with her that quickly.

'Jaghar?'

He jolted around. Vander had appeared in the doorway, no dukes anywhere near. A grim look of satisfaction lay on his mousy face.

'They heard it?' Jaghar said. His voice sounded too hoarse.

'Every bloody word of it.' Vander shut the door behind him and rubbed his face. 'Good gods. I never knew he was *that* much of a bastard.'

'No,' Jaghar said flatly. 'None of us, I think. How was their reaction?'

'Shocked, obviously. Pretty clear that they were listening to the man himself and that he really couldn't be talking about anyone's death but Trystan's. Eluard made the effort of thanking me for my warning when they left. Not a bad one, I think.'

'And Aldred?'

'Have seen thunderclouds looking happier.'

Jaghar grimaced. 'Alright. Might be reconsidering his vote, then. Could you go give Madelena a summary? With apologies for the delay.'

'What delay?'

He shrugged. No reason to tell Vander he had stormed out in the depth of night and never taken the time to send an update since. 'She'll get it.'

'Oh. Alright.' His man turned around, then hesitated. 'Jaghar – if you don't mind—'

'Hm?'

'That – *was* Rosin's voice, wasn't it?'

Jaghar closed his eyes. He'd hoped to avoid this, picked Vander as one of the few people who hadn't met Rosin more than a handful of times during her long years in his service. Turned out she was memorable enough even to people who hadn't fucked her.

'Better to forget that idea, will you?'

'But—'

'Vander.'

His spy caught the look in his eyes, abruptly shut his mouth, and swallowed. 'Yes. Alright. I'll let Madelena know the rest.'

'Thanks.'

The room remained icily silent after the door fell shut behind Vander's back. Jaghar sighed, turned around, and said, 'Yes?'

The tapestry flicked aside and Rosin stepped in, her hands on her hips, a triumphant grin on her heart-shaped face. 'Well. Smooth as a river pebble, wouldn't you say?'

He raised a cold eyebrow. She smiled even broader.

'I see you're not going to congratulate me?'

'Stop it, Rosin. You know better.'

'Do I?' She scowled, and even that gesture had an edge of triumph to it. 'Well, let's discuss the rest of the plan, then. You didn't forget what you promised me, didn't you?'

178

He averted his eyes. 'I—'

'Because,' she continued, 'I thought I should remind you that we aren't done with this yet. That is to say – I'm not done yet. Not that I assume you'd need the reminder, but—'

'What is your point?'

'Don't allow anything to happen to me, Jaghar.' Her smile was a knife stab, sharp and painfully precise. 'Don't allow me to get hurt. Don't leave me standing at the altar. Because I left a letter with someone whose name I won't mention, and if I don't personally stop him tomorrow, my friend will make sure that letter gets exactly to the people who need to see it. Don't think you want Aldred to hear during the Council meeting tomorrow that you've been screwing your little princess for months? Or that your bed isn't the only one where she's been spending her nights?'

The dismay rose in him with razor-sharp bitterness, a feeling of resignation rather than shock. He should have seen it coming. He should have known not to trust her, taken his precautions, made sure she wouldn't speak to a single living soul after his departure that night. Again he had failed, and again –

Again she was playing him.

'Get out.'

'Are you sure?' A coquettish hand on his arm; he shook her off like a stinging insect. 'I wouldn't mind staying around a little – it's been so long since I've...'

'Get – *out*.'

'Fine, fine...' She rolled her eyes. 'I'll see you at sunrise, then. Don't forget to inform the Temple that we're coming. Or do I need to—'

'Don't bother,' he interrupted her. 'I'll arrange things.'

'Unusually gallant. Perhaps you'll learn.' She again reached out a hand, then pulled back when his glare hit her. 'Enjoy your last unmarried night, then.'

He turned his back to her and heard her giggle behind him as she hurried off.

CHAPTER 13

Viviette left her mask and peignoir in the room, then waited for half an hour in her bedroom, sitting in her windowsill and staring out at the part of the courtyard she could oversee. No sight of Jaghar. If he had left the castle, he wasn't returning now.

A couple of hours.

She shouldn't expect him to be back already, she reminded herself every other minute. He had disappeared barely an hour ago. Gerald had been a far faster job than expected, there was no use in wasting her time on him if he'd agree with Aldred's vote no matter the circumstances – which left her with all the time in the world to sit here and wonder and hope and worry for the rest of the day...

She muttered a curse. There really wasn't much sense in waiting that long. But the nauseating tension in her guts lingered while she called for one of her girls to lace her back into her stifling black gown. What if he wasn't back by the time she returned to her room? What if he didn't return at all before nightfall?

She barely felt the corset squeezing her body back in line. Only when the girl interrupted her thoughts – 'Is that all, Your Highness?' – did she startle

'Oh, yes, thank you, Oda. You can go.'

'Are you very sure? I could help a hand with your hair?'

'No, no, that's alright. I'll do it myself for now.' The thought of hands plucking at her scalp for fifteen more minutes was unbearable – if only Jaghar had been around to help her... 'I'll call you for dinner if it needs some more attention by that time. Thank you.'

Oda still didn't disappear. With a rather desperate look on her round face, she continued, 'Anything to eat or to drink, then, Your Highness? You really look a little pale – my mother would say you needed a good glass of brandy to—'

'Oda, please.' Viviette sank down on the edge of her bed. 'You know I trust your mother's wisdom any other day, but I don't think brandy will do much for me now. Give it some time, will you?'

The girl curtsied. 'Yes, Your Highness. My apologies, Your Highness.'

'No, that's alright. Thanks for your concern.'

With another curtsy, Oda hurried off, closing the door behind her as if she tried not to wake a sleeping infant. Viviette closed her eyes for a heartbeat, then took up her hairbrush and began to braid her hair in the simplest style that would still be acceptable to the eyes of the court. A little pale. If only Oda's miracle recipe of warm brandy with honey and a slice of lemon could solve the problem of a dead father, sleepless nights, and a lover running amuck...

What if she left her room now and he showed up five minutes later?

She finished her braids, then pulled a sheet of scrap parchment from her desk and scribbled down a quick note – off to see a few dukes, she'd be back to check on this room regularly, please wait here. She folded it on her desk, put a clear *J* on it, and left it there in plain view. That should do. In the meantime...

Gerald's vote depended on Aldred, and Aldred's opinion likely depended on whatever evidence Jaghar could gather about her uncle's crimes. Which meant she had only one more duke to go –

Eluard.

Not enough to win her the Council if Jaghar couldn't manage to fix whatever he was trying to fix – gods be damned, why couldn't he just have *told* her what was going on? – but then again, a large minority might still be helpful to make any doubting duke reconsider his vote. And what else was she supposed to do? Look pretty and wait?

The room next to Wymond's, Madelena had said. If she knew where she could find Eluard, why in the world would she waste any more time?

She found no trace of Jaghar on her way to the guest tower. Her anger and worry kept her from hesitating; only when she already stood before Eluard's door, her fist raised to knock, did she pause. Two voices were arguing inside, loud enough for her to hear them even through a closed door.

Was that Aldred's voice, that sharp, snappy line interrupting the other every three heartbeats?

Viviette threw a quick glance over her shoulder and saw only the men Madelena had assigned to her, dutifully trailing after her. Fine. They'd know about the secret corridors already, and she didn't want to miss a moment more than necessary from the conversation inside the room...

She trotted back to the tapestry hiding the nearest entrance to Rock Hall's hidden network, a door she had used more than once to get to the rooms of clients assigned to her. Standing on her toes, she could just pry one of the lanterns from the wall. When she glanced over her shoulder, the warm metal clenched in her fist, her two guardians were eyeing her with obvious confusion.

'Don't think anyone will attack me in here,' she said, pushing her fingers into the narrow crack between the stones that hid the opening mechanism. The door opened without a sound 'You can return to my room. I'll see you there when I'm done.'

184

'But Your Highness...'

'Thank you.' She gave them a quick smile she didn't feel, stepped in, and closed the door behind her again.

She put down her lantern at the far end of the corridor so the shine wouldn't betray her. Then she tiptoed forward until she reached Eluard's room and examined the door – please don't let it be one of the more obscure opening mechanisms... But fate was kindly disposed to her for once these days: a rather obvious protruding stone in the right lower corner turned out to be all she needed to open it.

'... can't be *serious*!' a male voice that had to be Eluard's thundered into her quiet corridor, followed by an incredulous scoff. 'Did you hear the same words I heard? How in the world can you even *consider* voting in favour of a man who—'

'You're reacting too rashly!' Aldred interrupted, his voice croaking, but no less loud. 'I'm as unhappy to vote for a murderer as you are, but that doesn't make the alternative any less unlawful, and we can't—'

'He killed his *brother*, Aldred! And he's *gloating* about it! Is that really a man you want to put on a bloody *throne*!'

Viviette stood frozen, her hands suddenly trembling. They knew? They *knew*? Somehow two members of the Council had heard about Emeric's guilt – had heard it from the bastard himself? Was this Jaghar's doing? But how in the world...

'Are you even listening?' Aldred snapped. 'Of course I don't want him on a throne. He's a worthless boy and he has been for his whole life – but none of this is about what *we* want, do you understand that? The Council exists to make sure the laws are taken into account at every coronation, and according to the laws—'

'Murder is hardly lawful, is it?' Eluard said sharply.

'My point is that crowning an unmarried child isn't any more lawful!'

'Come on now – that's a *very* different order of magnitude. Being unmarried is a temporary issue. Being a murderer is quite a chronic—'

'The laws don't make a difference between—'

'Stop dragging on about your bloody *laws*!' Something shattered against stone, and Viviette flinched – had Eluard just thrown his mug against the walls in a fit of frustration? 'We're here for the common decency as much as for the laws, wouldn't you say? There's a reason they don't ask a judge to confirm the succession.'

'Even then...'

'She can be married within a month if need be! If it's what we need to keep some brother-murderer off a throne, I'll be overjoyed to look the other way for a couple of weeks and crown her by that time. The alternative—'

'Every man violating the law has a good reason to his own mind,' Aldred barked. 'We can't start that gliding scale in the very heart of the kingdom, for hell's sake.'

Eluard snorted. 'Well, I'll be happy to hear how you want to solve it, then. I hope the rest of the Council will be a little more sensible.'

'I'll staunchly discourage them from infringing upon our laws.'

'Yes, yes, of course you will, but I may hope you won't object to telling them what we heard?'

A short silence fell. Viviette was clutching her hands so tightly that she barely felt her fingertips anymore. Then Aldred growled a curse.

'No. We'll have to tell them.'

A wave of relief swept through her. Eluard sounded no less relieved on the other side of the tapestry.

'Good. Do you think we should write it down, with the memory still as fresh as possible?'

'May be a wise idea.' Aldred sounded annoyed to admit it. 'That servant boy should also be called as a witness, I believe – he's only a servant, of course, but he's the one who caught the first part of that conversation.'

A servant. Slowly the picture began to clear in her head. One of Jaghar's people calling the dukes towards a conversation in which Emeric confessed to his crime – but how in the world had that conversation ever come about in the first place?'

'There's the woman, too,' Eluard added, mere feet away.

A *woman*?

'Yes, but...'

'We have no idea who she is. No.' The sound of impatient footsteps pacing around the room. 'I don't know how we should find her either. We could ask the Spymaster. Perhaps he can figure it out?'

'I'd rather die than ask that Androughan for help,' Aldred snapped, and Viviette stiffened up behind the tapestry, a burning fury washing over her. That Androughan. If not for Eluard's clear indignation in his next sentence, she may as well have stormed into the room to give him an earful herself –

'Don't you think you're being a little ridiculous there, Aldred? We know Trystan trusted him, and as far as I know he's never—'

'And who says any spies even know her?' Aldred said, his voice growing louder again. 'She spoke about secret corridors of some kind, didn't she? If she used those to sneak into Rock Hall, I doubt even our omniscient Spymaster will have caught sight of her.'

'But then how does she know those corridors? She must have been here regularly to find them, wouldn't you say?' Eluard groaned. 'We could at least ask around – what did he call her again? Rosan? Rosin? Perhaps someone knows...'

Rosin!

Viviette staggered back, away from the door, clutching her hand over her mouth to smother the sounds of her squeaking breath. Around her, the world and the voices of the two dukes fell away as a memory of months ago pushed itself upon her again –

She's been obsessively in love with me for years...

And the story explained itself, rolling out before her mind's eye – Rosin, who knew the secret corridors after years in the masked service. Who could have sneaked into Rock Hall after their return two days ago, in some attempt to find Jaghar again. Who could have ended up listening to that meeting with her father and heard of his promise to name her his heir. Who could at least have suspected exactly what she'd do with the freedom to choose her own husband –

But would she really be cruel enough – desperate enough – to incite Emeric to murder only to prevent that wedding?

And did Jaghar know...

She closed her eyes. Oh, gods. His disappearance from the castle. His anguished expression of that morning. Suddenly it all made sense. He knew, yes –

Was *this* why he had been so reluctant to tell her?

The anger exploded within her in sudden, white-hot flares. He *knew*? Not such a complex story at all, a single mention of Rosin's name in that letter would have been enough of an explanation – and yet he'd kept silent? What did he think, that she'd crumble at the memory of his former lover? That she'd rather be ignorant and frightened than reminded of a rival who was never an actual threat to her?

Her hands trembled when she reached out to close the hidden door again – she didn't care about the two dukes discussing where they could find Emeric's mysterious accomplice, and damn all the laws Aldred thought were applicable in this particular situation. Where *was* he? If these two men had heard what they needed to hear, if the evidence was where it needed to be – why hadn't he come to see her yet?

Perhaps he was waiting for her in her room. She calmed herself with that thought as she stumbled through the hidden corridors, climbing narrow staircases and punching stones to open the doors on her way. But when she finally reached her own bedroom, it was empty, the parchment on the desk still folded.

Hell be damned.

Madelena's office? Empty as well, she found with a quick look inside. His own bedroom then? But she found even that sparsely furnished place deserted, the bed made, his leather jacket over the usual chair. He hadn't slept here for a long time. Now that she thought of it, he probably hadn't slept for a long time at all. Was he taking a nap somewhere? But then he should be in either of their bedrooms, not hidden gods-knew-where in Rock Hall.

With a muttered curse she sank down on his bed and buried her face into his blankets, inhaling the faint, musky scent of his body. A surge of hopelessness rose through her anger. Had he left the castle again – would she really have to wait for hours to find him? But Aldred and Eluard had their evidence, and unless he was arresting Rosin right now, he had no reason to stay away any longer...

So where else could he be? She rolled over in the blankets and tried to imagine what he'd be thinking. Exhausted, and lost and furious, betrayed by the woman who had spent so many years in –

The room of masks.

She scrambled up from his bed, a strange, hard certainty filling her limbs. The room. Of course, the room. The core of his service. The heart of his kingdom. Deserted until midnight. If there was any place where he could be hiding from the rest of the castle...

Any place where he could be hiding from *her*.

And she was running again, the flare of anger sending her feet over the irregular staircases with so much speed she may as well have been flying.

CHAPTER 14

A door slammed, far too close.

Light footsteps came closer at breakneck speed, audible only in the dead silence of Rock Hall's secret corridors. Jaghar somehow tore his eyes away from the heap of silk on the room's floor and jumped up from his heavy oakwood chest, expecting Rosin, or Madelena, or half an army for all he could care. Instead –

'Oh, *here* you are.'

Velvet came storming in like a river bursting through a dam, her green eyes burning with a fury he hadn't seen since he'd made the mistake of kissing her in Donovan's coach after saving her life. The skirts of her black dress were dusty, her hands clenched to fists.

For the shortest fraction of a moment he thought she might slap him in the face; then she abruptly came to a standstill mere feet away from him and snapped, 'Still busy with your *evidence*, I see?'

Her voice was heavy with a bitter sarcasm, her eyes shot lightning bolts at him. Jaghar stared at her, fighting his urge to crumble on the spot and never get up again. What in the world had happened? His letter? His disappearance from the castle? Or did she know – had she somehow figured out...

'So,' she added, without averting her piercing gaze for even the shortest moment. 'Rosin?'

Oh, demon be damned.

'How do you—'

'How do *I* know?' Her voice was rising. 'You're asking how *I* know? *You* knew what happened and you didn't even tell me?'

'Velvet, please – I'm sorry, I'm sorry, I—'

'You're *sorry*? You promised to come see me, you promised to explain it to me, and now I find you taking a good break in this bloody room instead of—'

'I was on my way to you!' he burst out, all fear and frustration and incomprehension shattering out of him – with his mind besieged by Rosin's letter and Emeric's knife and the neatly folded package of silk by his feet, how could he keep his voice down? 'I was coming to see you as soon as I was—'

'Then why are you...'

He swung an uncontrolled gesture at the floor. 'What in hell's name is *this*?'

She froze mid-sentence, blinked, then followed his hand with her eyes. The moment her gaze fell on the silk, her face turned blank, the colour draining from her cheeks in the blink of an eye.

Her peignoir – the peignoir he had never seen her wear except around the room. The dark blue silk mask on top. A mask that he knew had come from the chest on which he'd spent his last thirty minutes in nauseating bewilderment.

'Oh,' she said.

'Yes,' Jaghar said, twice as biting as intended. 'Hope you can imagine I was a little surprised?'

She opened her mouth, closed it again, then looked up. Her bitter laugh came a moment too late to pretend she meant it.

'Perhaps you shouldn't be disappearing without a trace for hours if you want me to ask for permission before—'

"*Permission*?' His voice soared up again, too loud for this smothering little room of velvet and mirrors. 'You think this is about *permission*? Doesn't occur to you that I'd be *worried* about you running off to screw people while there's a murderer on the loose? About what in the world you were thinking to jump into this work again while you're grieving your own damn father?'

'Oh, so you *really* wanted me to sit back and wait for hours?' she snapped.

'No! I wanted you to be safe, gods be damned! I don't want you to be hurt or upset or uncomfortable over *more* than your father dying and your uncle turning out to be a murderer, is that so...'

'That's why you didn't tell me about Rosin? Because it would *upset* me?'

Her voice cracked with those last words, and suddenly the fire flickering in her green eyes took on an entirely different meaning. Glaring at him, her arms wrapped around herself, her eyes gleamed suspiciously – not an expression of anger at all, now. Rather something that came very, very close to the look on her face when she had begged him not to be disappointed with her for wanting to marry him.

'Oh, please,' he managed, his voice coming down. 'You know better. I didn't expect you to collapse. I still don't expect you to collapse. You're still not weak, you're still not—'

'Then why didn't you bloody *tell* me?'

He sagged on the edge of the chest, burying his face in his hands. Even with his eyes closed, the memory of the knife in Trystan's back lingered before him. Velvet's silence was deafening. If even that razor-sharp mind didn't understand why he had hesitated to put the entire story in his letter...

'Do you even fully realise what happened?'

'She was the one listening to us that morning.' Her voice came out too flat. 'She told Emeric about Father's plan. And about the corridors too, I suppose? He used the corridors, didn't he?'

He nodded.

'Is there anything else to it?'

'Demon's sake – why do you think she did all of this?'

She was staring up at him when he opened his eyes, her face a pinnacle of confusion now. 'Because she's utterly deranged and hates me to death? Or is there anything else—'

'Velvet!' His voice cracked. 'Do you realise she did this – she sent Emeric after your father – because of *me*? If I hadn't been so blind to—'

'What in the world do you mean, because of you?'

'I should have *known*!' He spat out the words, the agony of the past night bursting out of him in a sudden flood of frustration. 'I *know* her, did you forget? I should have known she wouldn't just let me go. I should have known she wouldn't hesitate to sneak into Rock Hall again. I should have known she was willing to kill for...'

Her eyes grew wider. 'No – Jaghar – wait, that's not—'

'I about killed your father, for hell's sake!'

The words burst out of him like arrows, too loud and too sharp, leaving a wounded silence behind. There it was, the simple, painful truth – but she didn't move, didn't back away from him in justified disgust. She only stared at him with a blank face, the last of her frown dissolving.

"*That's* why you didn't just tell me?'

'Just tell you?' His voice was rising again. 'Should I *just* have thrown into your face that your father wouldn't have been dead without me? Do you hear how that sounds?'

'Good gods – will you stop?'

'Stop with what? I *did*—'

'Jaghar!' She jumped up, flinging her hand out at him as if to slam the sense into him. 'For hell's sake, you're far too intelligent to say such ridiculous things. I *told* you I don't blame you for this mess. Why in the world would you still think I'd think—'

'You didn't blame me for overlooking some threat neither of us knew,' he snapped. 'But that's not what this is, don't you see it? I could have known. I *should* have known. Demon's sake, I *did* kindly open the door for her and show her the way to that damned room, every unforgivable bit that...'

"*Unforgivable*?' Something was gleaming dangerously in the deep green of her eyes. 'Have you gone mad? What's the next step – are you going to tell me I'm supposed to despise you all of a sudden?'

'After I failed to do every single thing I'm paid to do?' He looked away and drew in a cold breath. 'Couldn't blame you.'

Her gaze burnt his skin in the silence that fell. There was something dangerous about the rhythm of her breathing, something ominous. Quick, shallow breaths, promising an eruption, a tension about to break. He didn't dare to turn and meet her eyes.

'No,' she said.

'What...'

Two steps, and she was close enough to throw herself into his lap and fling her arms around him. Her lips met his before he realised what was happening – a kiss like a punch in the face, fierce and brutal. He kissed her back out of pure reflex, nearly toppling over under the force of her fingers clawing into his sides. Only when his shoulders found the cold wall behind him did she pull back, out of breath and trembling.

"*Velvet*—'

'No,' she interrupted him, panting. 'Listen to me. Listen to me very carefully, because you're confusing things, and you need to stop confusing them very damn quickly – I am *not* your job, Jaghar. I didn't fall for your flawless track record, my heart is not some reward I'm paying you for your services – even *if* you failed at anything, even if you didn't do what you were supposed to do, that has absolutely nothing to do with the simple bloody fact that you mean more to me than the rest of this entire kingdom together. I'm not *firing* you. Do you understand me?'

Jaghar stared at her. His heart was pounding in every fibre of his body, a rush like being held at knifepoint, every inch of him focused on survival. 'But...'

'Oh, *gods*,' she said, closing her eyes. 'Jaghar...'

'You're not making sense.' Why did he sound like he was pleading? 'You're angry. You *should* be angry. Why wouldn't you...'

'Yes, of course I'm angry! So were you, in case you forgot!' She gestured at the pile of silk on the floor, so violently she nearly tumbled from his lap. 'Does finding that bloody mask mean you suddenly hate me from the bottom of your heart?'

He blinked. 'No, of course it doesn't, but...'

'See my damn point?'

'Velvet...' He groaned. 'I wasn't exactly *angry*.'

'Well, you ought to be,' she said, snorting. 'I was being reckless out of frustration. You should have opinions on it.'

Jaghar closed his eyes, unsure whether he wanted to ask the next question. He asked it nonetheless.

'Who did you—'

'Nobody.'

'Nobody?'

She curled against him, resting her face against his shoulder with a muffled curse. He felt the warmth of her breath through his shirt, coming a little too quick, and a little too shallow.

'Velvet...'

'I walked into Gerald's room, asked a few questions, walked out again before he could touch me.' She was speaking faster than usual. 'I suppose I was prepared for – no, frankly, I don't think I was.' A joyless chuckle. 'I could only think about you. About how much I wanted to leave – so I left. But I still should have talked with you before I did it.'

He wrapped his arms around her and slowly breathed out. Nobody. The relief curled through him with a cautious sensation of lightness, of comfort. Under the weight of her body in his lap, his senses abruptly seemed to realise how close she was, how warm, how beautiful.

'We didn't really talk about this, did we?' he muttered, holding her even tighter. 'The room? Others?'

Velvet shook her head in his arms, without looking up.

'Should we talk about it now?'

'It really should be pretty simple,' she said, still talking into his shirt. 'I don't want any others. I frankly have no desire to be Kara again. You can fling that bloody mask into the abyss if you'd like. So if you agree with...'

'You know I do.'

She lifted her head a few inches to kiss the skin just above his shirt – a quiet, feathery kiss, like the very first time she had touched him. 'Alright.'

He breathed in, very, *very* slowly, arousal and nervousness intertwining in his guts under the pressure of her body. Velvet looked up, a hint of mischief in the smile playing around her lips.

'And you still don't seem to hate me.'

'Demon's sake – of course I don't...'

'Can you stop that nonsense about never forgiving you, then?' she interrupted, pressing a brisk fingertip to his chest. 'You should be able to wrap your head around this, Spymaster. You're clever enough for it. If I do something stupid, you still love me, yes? Will you accept it's no different for me, then? Even if you run off every now and then without telling me why, there's still not another person in the world I'd want beside me on that bloody throne – it's that simple.'

Simple. *Simple*? The sound of the word trickled through him like warm water, soothing and reassuring. He *wanted* to believe her. He wanted so agonisingly badly to believe her – but he couldn't lie again, couldn't keep silent on the unpleasant details now...

'It's not just about me running off,' he said hoarsely. 'I caused more of a mess than that.'

Velvet tilted her head. 'Tell me.'

He hesitated, just a fraction of a moment. She heaved a slightly resigned sigh, raised her hands to his chest, and began to unbutton his shirt with such calm, nonchalant movements that it took him a moment too long to understand what was happening.

'Velvet, what are you...'

'You seem to be in dire need of some reassurance,' she said, continuing her work with a gaze of pure concentration. 'But don't mind me. Go on.'

'You—'

'Go *on*, Jaghar. I really don't want to give you orders anymore, but you're making it pretty damn hard this way.'

His shirt fell open. The unexpected sensation of her fingers against his naked chest sent a bolt of lightning through him, fire and ice in equal amounts; he sucked in a sharp breath and barely suppressed a curse. Velvet smiled at him. The blush on her face had deepened in the most disconcerting way.

'Velvet.' Inhale. Exhale. Slow, controlled. He had to keep his head clear. She really shouldn't forgive him this easily, he couldn't afford to make a single more misstep now. 'Velvet, you might want me to be a little more sensible for—'

'Considering the nonsense you've been uttering so far,' she said dryly, 'I doubt this is making you any *less* sensible. Go on.'

Jaghar closed his eyes. Her touches were slowly descending along the lines of his ribs, to the band of his trousers, a straight line towards his hardening desire. Hell's sake, why was he so easily defeated?

'Rosin,' he managed. 'She isn't exactly done yet.'

She carefully loosened the first button of his trousers. 'Am I supposed to be surprised?'

'What?'

If she wanted you enough to kill for it, of course she won't give up at once.' She stole a glance up at him as she pried loose the second button. 'What does she demand? Everlasting love? Marriage? A house full of babies? My head on a silver plate?'

A groan escaped him. With her fingers at his crotch and that strange, casual amusement in her voice, suddenly nothing seemed like much of a problem anymore. 'Only the marriage, so far.'

'Could be worse,' she muttered, and slid off his lap to kneel before him. 'And how is she planning to get you into the Temple with her?'

He opened his mouth to answer the moment she kissed his swollen tip, and the words he had wanted to speak dissolved in a mindless groan. She chuckled and flicked her tongue over his flesh. Jaghar grabbed the edge of the chest and squeezed his fingers into the wood. 'Velvet – please.'

She tilted her head so that his erection fell along her cheek and pressed a quick series of kisses to his shaft. It took all he had not to grab a fistful of her curls and shove himself between her lips – but he couldn't *again* pretend Rosin no longer existed...

'Go on,' Velvet murmured, dreamily running her lips along his length. He nearly crunched the wood under his hands.

'She's threatening to tell the Council about us. About your history as Kara, too.'

'Ah. That would definitely be unhelpful.'

'And...'

She finally parted her lips to take in the first inch of him. Sweet, wet warmth enclosed him, blissful and unbearable at once; gone were the room around him, the dukes determining the future of a kingdom, the deaths and murders of the past days... For a moment she was all he knew in the world, her tongue worshiping the aching head of his dick, her fingers cradling his sack, until even every threat Rosin had ever hurled at him dissolved in the fog of his lust.

Then, abruptly, she pulled back. A curse fell over his lips, and again she chuckled.

'So why didn't you kill her yet?'

'She's left some letter somewhere.' The words came out hoarse but easily, as if he hadn't spent hours on end wrecking his mind over them. 'Some friend who'll send it to the Council if she isn't seen alive tomorrow. I should never have—'

'You needed her to get the evidence, didn't you?' Velvet wrapped a slender hand around his erection. 'I think you did exactly what you should have done. You can deal with that friend.'

'But if...'

'Jaghar.' Again she slipped his tip between her lips. Her fist slid up and down his length with rough strokes that stirred pain and a burning lust in equal amounts. Jaghar closed his eyes – he *had* to keep his mind clear... But her voice seemed to come from miles away, muffled around his rigid flesh. 'Jaghar, you're the Spymaster of the Peaks. You handled dragons and witches and kings. You can deal with some bloody whore's friend too.'

He groaned. 'You make it sound so easy—'

'Because I already know you'll manage.' She pulled her head back, looking up at him with that same, rock-solid certainty in her green eyes, tender fingers massaging his erection until the building pressure of his arousal became nearly painful. 'And if you don't, we'll manage together. And if we don't, I'll still love you to death. Alright?'

How in the world was he supposed to think a single sensible thought with her fingers still tormenting him, driving him closer and closer to madness? Alright. It made no sense for things to be alright – but she wasn't a liar, and not a silly little girl he had to protect from her own decisions either – and if she wanted him, if she told him she wanted him –

'Are you sure?' he managed. 'Are you really sure...'

'You didn't kill him, Jaghar.' So calm. So unimaginably self-assured. He closed his eyes, feeling nothing but her hands on his scorching flesh and the hunger roaring through him, hearing nothing but her voice. 'She's trying to drive you mad again, trying to make you responsible for her own utter insanity. Even if you had done everything perfectly, she would still have found ways to betray you. I'm furious at *her*. Not at you. Can you please believe me on that?'

He parted his lips, then lost track of whatever words he had wanted to speak as she tightened her fist around his shaft and bent over to press a kiss to his tip. Long and hot and leisurely, her warm lips savouring the taste of him... He groaned and grabbed for the back of her head, tangling his fingers into her curls to press her closer.

A quiet sound escaped her at the touch, an involuntary moan of thinly veiled hunger – and Jaghar's last attempts at composure broke. With a sudden, nearly violent gesture he lurched forward and seized her from the floor, shoving her over the chest in the same movement. She grabbed his shirt and pulled him closer, laughing and out of breath.

'Believe me already, Spymaster?'

How could he *not* believe her? The rush of blood in his ears was deafening, loud enough to drown out even the most stubborn of his doubts. He grabbed for her skirts, pulled them out of his way and slipped his hand between her thighs, hungry for the warmth of her body, the tenderness of her touch. Her moan was all the encouragement he needed. When he ran a finger along her lips, she was as wet as if he'd spent the last hour pleasuring her.

'I must admit,' he muttered, flicking his thumb over that most sensitive spot beneath the dark curls, 'you don't give the impression there's anything problematic about—'

Velvet stopped his words with her lips, kissing him so passionately that he lost his balance and rolled beside her on the wooden chest, one arm still around her, one hand caught between her thighs. Caught in the warmth of her skirt his erection jolted, remembering the wicked sweetness of her mouth and yearning for more.

'Yes,' he whispered, pushing a first inch of his finger into her wetness. 'Yes, I'm starting to believe we may be alright, indeed.'

She let out another quiet moan. 'I'm happy to hear – really quite happy to hear...'

With a gravelly laugh he drew back his hand and rolled her on top of him so that she straddled him, sitting on his lower abdomen and covering his thighs and chest with her skirts. He glanced aside. The mirror on the other side of the room showed the tangle of their bodies, rumpled silk and naked skin and the shameless suggestion of what might be happening underneath that ladylike dress. When he came up on his elbows he found the same scene reflected at him in all five mirrors surrounding them, each of them showing the delicious lines of her body from a slightly different angle, each of them hiding the parts of her he craved to see most.

He groaned, grabbing her hips to lift her a few inches. 'Get those skirts out of the way.'

Velvet laughed and hitched up her skirts with hurried hands, baring her slender thighs. The mirrors behind her back showed every breathtaking inch of her, the marble mounds of her bottom and his straining erection sticking up between her legs, the tip prodding her soft flesh. An uncontrolled sound escaped his lips. Kneeling over him, Velvet uttered an elated, rosy giggle.

'Enjoying the view, Spymaster?'

She twisted her hips as she spoke, so that the swollen head of his dick slid along her wet lips and came to lie against her entrance, her muscles clenching against him at the touch. Again Jaghar couldn't suppress his moan. At the sensation of her warm, welcoming body, combined with the sight of his rock hard erection about to enter her, it took all he had not to grab her around the waist and fuck her senseless without another word of warning – but to fuck her he'd have to move, and to move he'd have to take his gaze away from the irresistible images the mirrors painted before his eyes.

'Hmm,' Velvet muttered as she leaned over to kiss him, revealing the pink secrets between her legs to the mirrors behind her, her glistening lips, the dark curls framing them. Jaghar felt her wet flesh slide over his shaft as he saw it, and barely felt her mouth against his forehead at the throbbing jolt of arousal that curled through him. He hissed a curse, clawing his hands into the edges of the chest to keep them off her body. Again she giggled, rubbing herself against his erection once more.

'Is that a yes?'

'Enjoying this torture?' he groaned, and she laughed.

'So much, Spymaster – so, *so* much...'

Slowly she angled her hips, allowing his tip to slide into her – less than half an inch into her tight warmth, then she pulled back again. Spellbound, he watched himself appear from her body, the pink head of his erection now glistening with her juices.

'Velvet...'

'More?' she said, her voice shimmering with temptation, and Jaghar uttered a breathless laugh.

'Please, more.'

Again she lowered herself onto him, just an inch at first, then slowly taking him deeper and deeper. 'Better watch closely, then...'

He watched. He watched like he had never watched anything in his life as he disappeared into her, lost himself in the warmth of her wetness, eyes and nerves screaming for priority in the flood of ecstasy that washed over him. At the sight of his own full erection invading her slender body, it seemed impossible, utterly unimaginable that she'd take him in entirely – and yet she didn't stop moving, receiving inch after inch of his hard length until she reached the base of his shaft. Only then did she come up again. He emerged wet and throbbing from her tightness, aching for release.

'More,' he breathed.

She obeyed, even slower now, gripping him so tightly that he thought for a moment he might faint at the sensation. Focussing his eyes on the sight of his glistening dick penetrating her, he clenched his hands to fists and forced himself to stay down, silent, sane –

With a sudden determination she impaled herself on him, burying his full length inside her, and Jaghar's last self-restraint evaporated into oblivion. With a curse he grabbed hold of her hips and lifted her a few inches, then arched up to thrust into her as he pulled her down again. She cried out, her knees tightening around his torso. At his second thrust her skirts escaped her grip, black silk tumbling down and obscuring his view on her delicate body and his steel erection taking possession of her. He paused, grinned.

'Get that dress out of my way, Velvet.'

She laughed and grabbled for her skirts, her breath heaving. Again he pulled her closer, driving himself into her faster and faster, building the unbearable tension in his groin to even more unbearable heights... She matched his rhythm flawlessly, coming down to meet him as he pushed up, arching her back to take him in deeper. Her moans grew louder as he fucked her, a siren's song luring him closer to the edge – until, without warning, the heat within him broke free and sent him spiralling into a blissful void, waves of pleasure washing over him and tightening every muscle in his body. Velvet rolled on top of him and tangled her fingers into his hair, kissing him with hungry, salty lips as the release rolled through him. Struggling for breath in between her kisses, he pressed her against his chest until his body stopped clenching and he was left spent and empty and, for the first time in days, *calm*.

'I hope you believe me now, Spymaster,' she whispered, giggling against his shoulder. 'If you need more convincing than this, I doubt either of us will survive.'

He let out a breathless laugh, rolling her on her back to lean over her. 'For both of our lives' sake... I'll just assume we're fine, then.'

'Wise.' She blew a dark curl off her face, ignoring the dozens of others that had escaped her braids, and sent a dazed grin up at him. 'Good gods. And now?'

Now. Something with dukes, and murders. A letter he still had to find, a kingdom he still had to save. But she already knew he was going to manage, and she lay soft and smouldering beneath him, and his hunger for her was far, far from satisfied yet.

'Now,' he said, kissing her forehead, 'I think I'm going to make you come screaming a couple of times.'

And then he proceeded to do just that.

CHAPTER 15

'I think we missed dinner,' Viviette muttered.

Next to her, without loosening his arms around her, Jaghar opened a single eye, threw a glance at the window of his bedroom, and smiled. 'Probably. Hungry?'

'You're going to joke about putting things in my mouth, aren't you?'

'You know me far too well, Velvet.'

She laughed and nestled her head on his shoulder again, running a finger along the white scars cut into his chest. Around them the mess of silk and linen, rough blankets and smooth furs bore testament to the madness of the past hours, their burst of passion on that hard wooden chest and the second round upon returning to his bedroom – a madness she could still taste sharp and briny on her tongue, shivering through her with every movement of his hands on her back and hips.

When she looked up, Jaghar was still lying back into the pillows, his eyes closed. The still smile on his face sent a fuzzy warmth through her intestines.

I'll just assume we're fine, then...

She leaned over to kiss him. He muttered her name and pulled her back against him, entangling her further in the mess of limbs and linen on his bed – there was no fighting his strength, and she gave in with only some laughing objections that his lips smothered at once. Only when he finally released her did she gather her breath again.

'Jaghar, if it's past dinnertime already...'

He opened a single eye again. 'I know.'

'The Council is meeting in less than twelve—'

'I know, Velvet. I know.' He groaned and released her to come up on his elbows. 'I'm just trying to forget about it.'

'If we forget about it they may pick Emeric.'

'Excellent occasion to run away and marry in secret before he can get his hands on you,' he muttered. 'How about Redwood?'

She couldn't help but laugh. 'Jaghar...'

'I'm joking,' he said, with a vaguely reassuring grin. 'Unless they actually pick him, of course. In that case you may expect me to drag you out of Rock Hall within an hour.'

'But then we have to leave the Peaks to *him*.'

'Yes.'

'We know what the Empress did to Cuvri. To Gennekha.' It didn't matter she had allowed herself to forget for a few blissful hours; the panic set its claws into her heart as though it had never been gone. 'If Emeric gets his way, her tax collectors may be starving the people within months after...'

'Velvet.' He sat up, rubbing his face. 'You don't need to tell me.'

She swallowed the rest of her sentence, pulling her knees to her chest and wrapping her arms around them. No, she didn't need to tell him. If anyone knew what the Taavi Empire was capable of... But the idea of fleeing Rock Hall like a thief in the night, of leaving the Peaks in the hands of the man responsible for the knife in her father's back – how would she bear the thought even if she managed to escape?

'Listen,' Jaghar said, his voice pressing. 'We can figure this out. You have Wymond's vote and Laudine's vote. Aldred and Eluard know Emeric is the king's murderer. That should make—'

'Aldred believes putting a murderer on the throne is as illegal as putting an unmarried woman on the throne,' she said bitterly.

He blinked. 'How do you know?'

'Listened to their conversation – Aldred and Eluard. How do you think I figured out about Rosin?'

'Ah.' He grimaced. 'Explains a little. And Eluard?'

'Isn't voting for Emeric. Was of the opinion that they might as well crown me and marry me off within a month or some construction of the kind. But that would at least be a month of respite.'

'So that's three votes. If one of the others – well, not Gideon, probably, and we shouldn't count on Osric either – but if Gerald—'

'Gerald,' Viviette said, closing her eyes, 'will probably be voting whatever Aldred votes.'

'What?'

'Wants to marry Aldred's daughter. Said some smug things about showing Aldred that they were of one mind when it came to politics and law.' She looked up again and grimaced. 'Didn't really feel like staying around and making an attempt to change his mind.'

He breathed out a little too slowly. 'How much of a problem would it be if I carved a few lines into his face, you think?'

'I would acquit you without hesitation, but that's probably not what you were asking.'

'Afraid it isn't.' He groaned. 'What a bloody spineless fool. So we need to get Aldred to our side?'

'I suppose so, yes.'

He muttered a curse. 'Well. There is a chance we don't need to do it ourselves, of course. The Council will discuss the arguments before they cast their votes. I suppose Wymond and Laudine will do their best to convince the bastard, especially when they hear Emeric is responsible for both the king and Reginald.'

'But still – if they don't manage...'

Jaghar closed his eyes. She waited a long, silent minute before she added, 'Jaghar?'

'I don't know,' he said, averting his face. 'And – as little as I want to think about it – I'm not sure how much time I'll have tonight. I still need to get out of a marriage.'

A flare of fury shot through her – not at him, but at the red-headed woman she had met only once, on the night that had nearly seen her killed in Mauno's room. Marriage. Gods be damned. Why don't you let me handle it, she nearly wanted to say, I'll be overjoyed to shove the bitch into the abyss in your name. But she ought to know better – if any mysterious letters were still hiding in town, she wasn't the person to solve that problem.

'Alright,' she said instead. 'So you handle Rosin and I handle the Council?'

'Sounds lovely,' he said wryly. 'Any plans?'

'Not yet, unless you consider killing Osric and Gideon in their sleep a plan.' She sighed. 'I'll come up with something. Or I'll just beg Wymond to make a damn good case and convince Aldred somehow. In any case – leave it to me. You need to focus on that letter.'

Jaghar examined her for a few long heartbeats, his dark eyes strangely soft. Then he averted his gaze, pulled her clothes off the floor, and began to untangle the ribbons he had so carelessly yanked loose hours ago.

'Will you be careful?' he said.

'I always am.'

'Will you be even more careful, then?' He looked up, beckoning her closer to slide the dress over her head. 'Emeric will have noticed our absence during dinner. He knows what we know – if he suspect's you're up to something...'

For a moment the world drowned in black silk and the smell of her own arousal lingering in the dress. When she emerged into the twilight again, Jaghar looked no less concerned.

'I'm not planning to go anywhere near Emeric,' she said, and he raised an eyebrow.

'Are you planning anything, then?'

She quietly turned around so that he could strap down her bodice again, with strong, skilful fingers. Did she have a plan? Thoughts were itching at the back of her mind, vying for her attention like spectators at a crowded event pushing to the front – but they were loose shreds of memories and observations that could barely go for plans. Marriage and the Temple, the High Priest and his wandering hands, her father's last living smile and the cold metal of a signet ring pressing into her hand palm...

'I – I'll have to think.'

He dressed himself, then pulled her back into his arms and held her in silence for minutes, slowly running his fingers through her hair while the room darkened around them. Viviette knew she ought to be frightened. She knew she would be, too, as soon as he was gone – while he was downtown trying to find a letter that might reveal their secrets to the world at the most disastrous moment, while the weight of her kingdom's future rested on her shoulders entirely. But in the brewing warmth of his embrace, not even those alarming thoughts could stir up the fear again; his presence alone smothered all panic she ought to have felt.

'Well,' he said eventually, releasing her and stepping back. In the twilight, his face was an unreadable mask. 'I suppose I'll go, then.'

'Yes.'

I love you, she wanted to add. I want to win this fight even if I win it for you alone. I want you beside me if they ever allow me on that throne – I want you to be mine and mine alone, and I want the world to know it, too. But he knew, already. They both knew. And if they didn't come out of this night alive, it wouldn't make any difference at all.

'Stay safe,' she said, and a faint smile slid over his face.

'I'll still take that as an order, Princess.'

She watched him leave from his own bedroom window, his slender figure barely visible in the shadows as he crossed the courtyard and disappeared through the castle's main gate. Then she turned away from the window, away from him, and sank down on his messy bed, burying her face in her hands.

The Council.

Three votes in her favour. Two votes against her. Two dependent on Aldred's interpretation of her kingdom's inheritance laws – but how could she ever hope to influence that interpretation if he hadn't even been persuaded to take a slightly milder approach in his own nephew's favour?

She muttered a curse. Gerald, then – was there any hope he might go in against his intended father-in-law after all? But the young man hadn't seemed much aware of the existence of his own spine, and a single night was woefully short to make him give up his hopes of a marriage to Lady Athelina...

What other options did she have? Gideon? His derisive grin had told her enough – he'd laugh in her face. Osric? The man needed a king with favourable opinions towards the Taavi if he didn't want to rot in some prison cell for the rest of his life. Emeric offered him as much as a guaranteed acquittal – the duke would be a fool to vote for anyone else.

She fell back into the blankets and closed her eyes. Come on, Velvet. *Think*. A murderer versus an unmarried woman. What did she have to tilt the balance in her favour? An informal engagement to an Androughan Spymaster? Highly unlikely that would convince anyone, Aldred least of all. A father intending to name her his heir? He *hadn't* named her his heir, and to Emeric's side, that would be all that mattered. Gods be damned – if only she had accepted Jaghar's joking proposal to marry in some small Redwood Temple along the road back home...

Her eyes flew open.

This was what her mind had been trying to tell her – what, perhaps, part of her had wanted to do since that impulsive moment in Reginald's office. With a hammering heart she jumped up, her hands suddenly restless and fidgety. She had a plan. An actual *plan*. Now she only had to be quick, and clever, and careful enough to survive the night –

But what choice did she have?

CHAPTER 16

I *left a letter with someone whose name I won't tell you.*
Jaghar stood still in front of the lodging house, staring at the stag's head above the door without seeing much. His fists itched with an urge to burst in, draw a knife and threaten her until she'd simply tell him where she left that bloody letter – but she knew far too well that he couldn't *actually* hurt her as long as that deadly information about the past months still out somewhere, and that he could most definitely hurt her by the time he found it... Threats wouldn't help him. He had to be more clever than that, even if his whole body was screaming for quick, brutal revenge...

You can deal with some bloody whore's friend, Velvet had told him, and he almost flinched – because what if he couldn't? What if he disappointed her? Then, just as quickly, an unexpected, unusual calm came over him, washing away even the smouldering anger in his limbs. What if he couldn't? He'd have to flee Rock Hall. He'd have to beg Tamar for a place to stay. But Velvet would forgive him, would still love him too, because she wasn't a job and he wasn't some servant she paid for his service – which meant that he would survive...

And all of a sudden, everything was crystal clear in his mind.

Rosin had left a letter with someone she knew well enough to trust that it would indeed be delivered if she didn't show up as a married woman tomorrow morning. But that wasn't all. *Don't think you want Aldred to hear during the Council meeting that you've been screwing your little princess...* During the Council meeting. She knew the court. She knew the average prostitute or tavern owner couldn't storm into Rock Hall during that ceremony and demand to be heard by the seven most powerful people of the kingdom. Which meant that she had found someone else. Someone who could speak without getting dragged out of the castle. And she really didn't have too many friends of such a position...

She did have her clients, however.

He slowly turned away from the house, his eyes swerving over Mine Street and the town beyond. Of course. She had never devoted every night to the work in Rock Hall – had still visited the regulars from the time before he asked her to join his ridiculous plan. The owner of the Mean Cat, at the more expensive end of Mine Street. The glassblower of Brewer Street. And –

Rolland. The goldsmiths' guild master.

Jaghar closed his eyes as the thought unfolded in his mind, pieces of the puzzle clicking together at every turn. The man had been one of her most regular clients for nearly a decade. He knew the court. Hadn't Rosin herself once joked that she could learn as much about Rock Hall's inhabitants in Rolland's bed as in the room of masks itself? And even the most arrogant of dukes would probably listen to the man who controlled where their gold coins came from...

The plan forming in his mind, he began to walk.

He was ready by sunrise, prepared for the last step of his plan and so strangely calm that it seemed an entirely different man came striding onto Mine Street in the early morning light. He had trouble remembering how he had kicked in that thin wooden door, as if the incident happened two years rather than a single night ago – as if it hadn't been him at all. Had the traces of his own feet not still been visible below the lock, he might have believed the entire episode only existed in his imagination.

The stocky woman who opened the door for him certainly hadn't forgotten, however, judging by the scowl that grew upon her face as she recognised him.

'What do you want?'

'I suppose Rosin is at home?' he said, raising an eyebrow.

She looked like she was about to deny it just to annoy him, but Rosin's voice interrupted before she could speak, coming from the top of the stairs in a cheerful tone that nearly broke through Jaghar's carefully created layer of stoic composure.

'It's fine, Sira! He'll be leaving with me in a moment.'

Sira's scowl deepened, but she turned around without further objections, muttering quiet words of disapproval as she stumbled back up to her room. Rosin came dancing off the stairs a moment later, her green dress fluttering around her ankles, her smile a strange mixture of playful mockery and genuine excitement. Jaghar locked the air in his lungs and stood still. At least if he didn't move, he wouldn't accidentally punch that same smile off her face.

'You came!' she said breathlessly as she pulled the door shut behind her.

Of course I damn well came, he wanted to say. You threatened the right people, or better, exactly the wrong people; it doesn't matter I'd rather die than spend my life with you, because even this marriage would still be preferable to robbing Velvet of her throne. He swallowed his words. There was no use in keeping her on guard, in betraying that he was still fighting her strings pulling him.

'Yes.' He forced himself to hold out an arm and not flinch as she laughed and slipped her hand through. 'I've been thinking. Figured out a couple of things.'

Rosin gave him a side glance, her smile still uncomfortably bright, but now with a hint of curiosity. He purposefully didn't turn to meet her gaze, and she gave in within half a minute of walking.

'So what did you think about?'

He raised an eyebrow, glancing at the dealers, whores and gamblers passing by. 'That's not a conversation I'd prefer to have with the entire criminal population of town listening along, if you don't mind.'

'Why would they listen to you!'

'Why wouldn't they?'

She gave a playful tug at his arm, the curiosity shamelessly obvious in her voice now. 'Well, then we'll take another route – you won't avoid telling me, Jaghar.'

'Can't we talk about this at another—'

'No.' She released his arm and took two steps away from him, in the direction of the centre. Not the direction where he needed her. 'Come on, we can go—'

'The market squares won't be much more silent,' he interrupted, nodding at the side street to his right. 'We can take this way, if you *must* speak about it.'

She was already coming after him, looking utterly triumphant. Jaghar forced himself to produce something close to a smile as they stepped into the deserted alley, which was so narrow that the sunlight never reached the sand of the street. These houses were the last of the town, built mere yards away from the abyss; behind them there was only the path running along the edge, leading to the protruding cliff half a mile away on which the Temple was built. Rosin grabbed his arm as soon as they emerged from the alley, squinting against the bright orange sunlight that flooded the grassy rocks and the mountain tops lining the horizon.

'So,' she said, cheerfully. 'No excuses, anymore. Tell me what you've been thinking about.'

'Love and life.' He raised an eyebrow. 'As one is supposed to do on a wedding day, I believe.'

'You're *teasing* me.'

He closed his eyes for the shortest fraction of a moment. Teasing her. Did she think this was a game, a silly joke rather than a deadly plot that had killed or threatened every single person he loved in the world?

'It struck me,' he said, 'that perhaps I've been misunderstanding the whole concept of love all this time.'

He kept his voice flat, his eyes deliberately away from hers. Her sharp inhalation still didn't escape him.

'See,' he added, walking on in the same brisk pace, 'I've always been under the impression that love was something you ought to deserve. Perform well, and perhaps you'll be worthy. Fail, and prepare to lose it again. Quite a frightening perspective. I'm sure you can imagine.'

'Of course I can.'

She sounded eager, nearly hungry for his words. He looked away and forced his breath to slow down despite the pressure pulsing through his veins, the tension speeding up his heartbeat – not yet. Not now. But before them the Temple loomed up already, pillars and arches rising from behind a sharp granite ridge, and the sight of it alone left his mouth painfully dry.

'Jaghar?'

'Turns out,' he said curtly, 'that I may have been wrong.'

'And what made you realise...'

'The right woman loving me, I suppose.'

This time she stayed silent as they walked on, further and further away from the edge of town. From the corner of his eye, he could see her stare at him with an expression of elated, nearly euphoric triumph.

'A strange thing to realise so suddenly,' he continued. It was easy now. There was no lie to it anymore. 'That it may not even matter how many times I mess up. That it may be fine if I speak the wrong words every now and then and do the wrong things every now and then – that I can make honest mistakes and acknowledge them and apologise. That someone who truly loves me will forgive me – just like I'd never hold honest mistakes against anyone I love.'

She halted beside him, clutching her hand over her mouth. 'Jaghar!'

He turned to face her. A few hundred yards behind her the last houses lay still in the morning mist, glowing in the light of the rising sun to nearly the colour of her abundant red curls. Beside them, quiet and waiting, the abyss.

'Jaghar – do you mean – can you forgive me for...'

'If I'm honest,' he said, reaching for her with both hands, 'I'd happily kill for the woman I love.'

She opened her mouth, but didn't speak as he took her hands and pulled her towards him, locking his arms around her without releasing her wrists. The scent of her alone, so close to him, made his stomach turn, but he didn't waver; clenching her hands against her back, her body caged between his arms, he lowered his face to her ear and continued, 'The problem, Rosin...'

For a heartbeat nothing in the world moved, not even her curls in the morning breeze. He looked up, and sighed.

'The problem is you're not that woman.'

She tried to jolt back but didn't manage; his arms around her were a vice, locking her against his chest with barely even room to breathe. Her breath quickened with alarm and confusion. 'What in the world...'

'It's really taken me far too long to realise it,' he said, clenching his fists even tighter around her struggling wrists – he wasn't supposed to enjoy this, but he remembered the sight of the knife in Trystan's back, the emptiness in Velvet's eyes as she cried in his arms, and couldn't suppress the grim satisfaction welling up in him. 'And perhaps I only truly realised it last night – what you did to me. What games you played with my mind. How you reminded me at every possible occasion of the man I feared I was – how you made me believe I was indeed that monster if I didn't adhere to your wishes... Your forgiveness was the opposite of forgiveness. It was a weapon. And you'd damn well have made me believe it, too, if not...'

She was trying to yank her arms from his grip now, her breath rasping through her throat.

'... if not for her,' he continued, undisturbed. 'And I want you to hear me say this, Rosin. I want you to understand exactly what she is, because you hurt her, you hurt me, and this is all the revenge I'll ever get – I love her. I love her like I've never loved you or anyone else in the world. I would die for her and die a happy man, and you'll never get it – because she doesn't try to own me. Because she doesn't claim a right to me. Because she only needs to be here and love me, truly unconditionally, and that's enough to make me hers until time itself stops turning, do you understand?'

'Jaghar, please!' Her voice was rising to shriller and shriller heights. She must feel the threat in his quickening breath, his tightening fists. She must know where his steps forward were pushing her. 'Stop – you've lost your mind – I've written a letter! I've written a letter and the Council will know—'

'Should have hidden it better,' he snapped, pressing her another step closer to the edge.

'No! No, please – Jaghar, no, you can't hurt me like that – I *love* you, I promise. Everything I ever did was...'

'Out of love?' He stood still, unable to suppress a biting laugh. 'You killed the man I loved like a father. You hurt me more than you'd have hurt me by sticking that damned knife into my own back, and you still think you were doing it out of *love*?'

'I just wanted you to—'

'Exactly. *You* just wanted.'

'But...'

He shoved her away from him, his fingers still locked around her wrists. She was trying to kick him in the shins, her curls a messy veil over her contorted face. '*Jaghar*!'

'Say hello to Mauno from me,' he said, and pushed.

For a moment she hung frozen in the air, tilted back over the edge of the chasm, her arms wide as if she was still waiting for some hero to jump in and catch her –

And then she was gone into the swirling mist of the depths below, leaving nothing but a last shrill cry behind.

CHAPTER 17

Mine Street at night was cold and noisy, and smelled like rot and bodily fluids Viviette didn't even want to think about.

Her woollen cloak covered most of her – enough, at least, to hide the silk dress underneath from view. But the biting mountain winds came sneaking through at every gust, and with one hand clenched around her small knife and one fist closed around her father's signet ring, she didn't have limbs left to pull the wool tighter.

But perhaps it was rather the fear that left her shoulders shaking so uncontrollably.

Around her, the world was creeping up at her from the shadows and the corners of her eyes; whenever she turned her head to a sudden movement in the periphery of her view, every threat turned out to be empty – just some women slinking by or a drunk stumbling out of an alley. And yet this was still Mine Street... She should have taken the alternative way, of course, the path leading along the abyss. But the thought alone brought up the memory of Mauno's scream dying away in the distance, and she'd rather face the entire underbelly of town than the strange glowing depths of the abyss at night...

'Hey!' a voice hissed behind her, far too close, slurred and lisping. 'You – girl!'

Viviette snapped around. A young man came limping up, examining her like a merchant inspecting his wares. Before she could speak a word, he continued, smirking like a hyena. 'Three copper coins? And a beer, if I like you?'

She wanted to run. She wanted to scream. Instead she thought of Jaghar, his cold, silent threats that could silence even the worst of troublemakers –

'I'd advise you to get away from me.'

Her voice came out too level for her trembling shoulders. It barely sounded like her own voice at all. The other's smirk dwindled.

'Oh, are we going to play—'

'I'm not playing,' Viviette cut in, her fingers nearly squeezing through the smooth, cold steel of her knife. He was drunk, she told herself. Drunk and unarmed.

Even unpractised, she had the upper hand here. 'I'm not for sale. You have no business with me. Get out of my sight before I start getting more unpleasant about it, will you?'

Suddenly he no longer looked nearly so drunk, with his shrewd dark eyes scanning her face for a trace of jest, a moment of weakness. Viviette stared back. Like Jaghar, the voice in the back of her mind repeated – don't move, don't blink, don't smile. Just know, and know it hard enough to make them understand it too, that *you* wouldn't be the one in trouble if they decided to be stupid.

The man muttered a curse and turned away from her with a last vulgar gesture. Only after a few heartbeats did she dare to believe he wouldn't abruptly change his mind – and even then her cramped fingers didn't let go of her knife.

She didn't catch sight of Jaghar anywhere as she hurried on past the shabby establishments and the cheap lodgings, hiding in the shadows where she could. A good sign, hopefully, or at least it may mean he was doing something – and even if it didn't, there was no sense in worrying about that now. He could handle his part of the work. At least he could survive it. She should focus first on making sure he wouldn't come home to her empty bedroom tomorrow morning and find only the note she had left on her desk for him.

A drunken brawl arose to her left, and suddenly men were shouting and swinging fists all around her, missing her by mere feet as she ducked away into an alley and waited for them to pass. Her heart hammered in her throat. Perhaps she *should* have taken one of her father's knights along after all – but then again, a man in full armour would have drawn an unpleasant amount of attention, too, and worse...

Someone would have known where she was going. Someone might have guessed what she was about to do.

She managed to circumvent the fight and escaped another man who listed a rather extensive list of demands before offering her two copper coins for her services. Then finally Mine Street was behind her, and only a few more respectable, silent streets still lay between her and the Temple. Now, with no glaring eyes on her anymore, she ran, coat fluttering around her, feet stumbling over the uneven sand path – midnight was approaching, and this night was the only chance she had... The Temple loomed up from the darkness before her as an ominous, brooding giant, a colossus of broad granite pillars shielding the inner rooms from view. She had seen it at night before, at midsummer and midwinter celebrations, but then there was always *some* light – lanterns lining the road, the occasional fire basket on the gallery. Now it gave the impression that no living soul dwelled inside.

'Halt!' a loud voice bellowed, and Viviette slipped to a standstill. A broad man emerged from the shadows between the building's pillars. In the faint light of the moon above them, she couldn't distinguish more than his chainmail and the silhouette of a sword at his belt.

'Evening,' she said, lowering her hood.

The guard hesitated at the sound of her voice, or at the sight of her long braids. 'Who in hell are you?'

'Messenger for the High Priest,' Viviette said. 'From Rock Hall.'

'Why in the world would Rock Hall send a bloody girl—'

'That's something I'll discuss with the High Priest, if you don't mind.'

He snorted. 'Look, every lass can storm in and claim she's some messenger – the midnight fire is about to be lit, I can't—'

Viviette stuck out her hand, her father's signet ring in her open palm.

'What's that?'

'The king's signet ring. In case you doubted whether I'm indeed representing the family.'

He stepped closer, bringing with him a smell of mulled wine and sweat so strong that Viviette nearly flinched. His thick fingers picked the ring from her palm with surprising care.

'That's – the king's seal.'

'It is, indeed. Can I pass? It's rather urgent.'

He planted the ring back into her hand and gestured her to walk on with a muffled curse. 'Don't disturb the fire.'

'Wouldn't dare,' Viviette said, hurrying past him.

Only as she approached the building did she catch the shine of a single lantern on the wall – just enough light to show her the entrance. With her hands against the rough granite walls, she tiptoed on, inhaling the scent of dust and incense. Nearly midnight. Which meant Hamond was preparing the ritual, and that one of the Temple girls should be building the pile of wood for his midnight flame...

She unbuttoned her cloak and slipped out of the warm wool in a shadowy corner of the first room. Her silk Temple dress barely held out the cold, but at the very least the wind didn't blow between these massive walls.

And at least she *had* a Temple dress. What would she do without the accessory chests in the room of masks?

She left her knife with the cloak and walked on with only the ring still clenched in her fist. Two silent rooms; then, finally, the sound of wood against wood. When Viviette glimpsed around the doorway, a tall blonde girl in an identical silk dress was just laying a new log on the sprawling pyre she had built on the altar.

'Can I interrupt you for a moment?' Viviette said.

The girl shrieked and jumped around, then cowered away from the door. 'Who – who are—'

'Listen, I can't explain this now.' Not with midnight approaching fast – but then again, would she be able to explain it at any other moment? 'I need to take your place for tonight. Orders from someone in Rock Hall. Don't worry, you didn't do anything wrong, but there's something they want to know.'

A slight blush stole over the girl's face. 'Is it – is it about Hamond?'

'I can't say anything about it yet. Just leave me alone with him. Here.' Again her signet ring did the dirty work for her. 'This is the king's seal. I'm here with royal orders, do you see?'

'Oh, good gods. I – I see – I'll leave, then – where do you want me to go?'

'Wherever you'd normally go after the flame is lit.'

The girl nodded and swallowed, throwing a quick glance at the pyre. 'You – eh – I hope you know that he might – eh...'

Viviette nearly finished that sentence in a wording that might send any good Temple servant fainting. The bastard, putting his hands on girls who barely knew the words for what he did to them... 'Yes. I know.'

'Oh. Are you...' She swallowed again. 'Sorry. I won't ask questions. Eh – good luck?'

'Thanks,' Viviette said, with a small smile. 'Be off now, will you?'

The girl stole away like a thief in the night, with what looked suspiciously like an expression of relief. Viviette considered running back to get her knife anyway – why not welcome the High Priest like he deserved? But there was more at stake than the Temple's honour tonight, and a knife wouldn't be the most diplomatic way of saving it...

So she waited, with her back towards the door from which she knew Hamond would arrive, staring at the pyre before her.

Midnight announced itself with the faint blaring of trumpets in the distance. The footsteps behind her back approached a moment later, slow and heavy.

Viviette waited, unmoving. From the other side of the room Hamond walked closer, with that dramatic, heavy tread she had seen him use at the celebrations as well – every step intended to shake the very earth itself. He didn't speak until he was mere yards behind her. A dull thud of ceramic sounded against the granite floor when he put down the vessel holding the burning candles.

'Well, well.'

She had only heard that deep voice in chants and speeches, when he always spoke with immense gravitas. Now there was something strangely casual to his words.

'I see we have a new acquisition to welcome to the family?'

She bowed her head without speaking. He chuckled behind her.

'There is no reason to be shy, my dear girl. You built an excellent pyre. I'd believe you've been doing it for years – come, turn around, let me see your face.'

Viviette didn't move. Again he laughed.

'Is it the fear paralysing you? Ah, yes, I can imagine, your first time doing the ceremony – but don't worry, you'll learn soon enough that we prefer to be a little less formal at the Temple when nobody is watching us.'

With one more step he was standing close behind her and laid his hands on her hips. Through the thin silk of her dress, the warmth of his body was an immediate relief on her icy skin – but the kind of relief that made her want to twitch away. She stayed frozen where she was, and he muttered something appreciative.

'No objections? Very well, my dear...'

Viviette held her breath as his fingers tread on over the smooth silk, climbing along the curves of her body. One more moment. Allow him to tread into slightly more unforgivable territory – let him dig the grave a little deeper... He found the onset of her breasts and curled his fingers around them with thinly veiled impatience.

'I suggest you stop there, Hamond.'

Her voice sounded strangely loud in the dead silence of the night, and he froze, still cupping her breasts, his panting too fast and too heavy with desire.

'And take your hands off me,' Viviette added briskly.

He pulled back his hands as by reflex. 'Who – what in the world?'

She turned around, one eyebrow raised. Hamond stumbled back as if she had slapped him in the face, nearly stumbling over his flame; above his strong, straight nose, his eyes were wide enough to pop from their sockets any moment.

'Your – Your *Highness*?'

'And a good evening to you, too,' Viviette said with a cold smile. 'Strange way to greet a Temple virgin, I must say. Sounded like you're making a habit of it, too.'

'I – what in the world?'

'Defamation of holy grounds, I believe? If I recall correctly, they put a man's head on a pole for taking a piss in this room when I was five or six years old. I'm not sure how fondling innocent girls compares, but at the very least—'

'Look,' he interrupted her, his deep voice unusually high, 'this is a misunderstanding, Your Highness – I can explain – you see, I thought you – you were...'

She tilted her head. Under her look of genuine interest, his sentence came to a stammering halt. He thought what? Even if he had believed her his mistress, or a goddess descended to bless him, or a scarecrow for all she cared, his intentions had been clear.

'At the very least,' she continued when he stayed silent, 'removal from all public offices will be the first step. I hope you have some savings at hand – assuming, of course, that you won't be fined to reimburse those poor girls for—'

"*Please*!' His face had gone ashen in the flickering candlelight. 'I didn't want – I didn't mean to – please, Your Highness, isn't there anything I can do...'

Again his voice trailed away into nothingness. Viviette gave him a radiant smile.

'Well, now that you remind me, there may actually be a little something you could help me with, Hamond.'

He closed his eyes, looking about to faint. 'Please – forgive me – anything I can do—'

'Excellent,' Viviette interrupted, stepping back and folding her arms. 'Then please light that bloody fire and show me the way to your office, will you? We have some work to do tonight.'

CHAPTER 18

The hall was already filling up when Jaghar walked in, the whispers of the audience infusing the air with a tense sensation of breathlessness.

It took him a moment to make sense of the set-up of the room. Nothing stood in its usual place: the chairs and benches were placed in semicircles around the throne and the table at the far end of the hall, so that Rock Hall resembled a monstrous theatre, the Council meeting merely a play for the amusement of its audience. He swept his gaze over the crowd. For an instant he only found nobles and knights, and an explosive dread slammed through him – wasn't she here? Had something happened last night? Had she made one clever plan too many?

Then he found her, sitting at the front row in black velvet – shoulders hunched, fists clenched in her lap, but undeniably alive. For the first time since he had left her behind last night, his shoulders relaxed a little.

And now?

He wanted to walk up to her, sit down beside her, and tell her what had happened, what he had done – he wanted to ask about her night, any brilliant solutions she might have come up with. But she was sitting in full view of the court, and a dozen people at least would be trying to listen along with every word they spoke...

So instead he slipped around the back of the audience and moved to the front on the more silent side of the hall, taking care to stay in the shadows. Even there Velvet noticed him within a minute, turning to him with every single question written out in her eyes. She looked far too pale. She looked strangely triumphant, too.

He gave her his quickest smile. The corners of her mouth perked up for the shortest moment before she turned back to the long table before her.

The table where seven silent figures were sitting already, waiting for the meeting to begin.

Jaghar leaned against the wall and let his gaze slide over them. Wymond, leaning back in his chair with crossed legs and folded arms, his eyes scanning the public without pause. Osric, thin and sinewy, licking his lips every other heartbeat and throwing nervous glances at the knights surrounding the table. Laudine, her back stiff and her lips a straight line, staring at her own gloved hands on the table before her. Aldred, scowling at everybody who accidentally stepped too close to the table, clenching a few parchment leaves in his blotched hands. Gerald, perched up in his chair, glancing at the old duke to his side whenever he moved a finger. Eluard, the youngest of the group, rubbing his face every moment with a look that suggested he'd be happy to wake from this strange dream. Finally, Gideon, the only one not dressed in black, smirking at every familiar face in the public as if he were sitting at some village dancing fair rather than the Council of the Peaks.

Most of them didn't even nod to greet Emeric as he finally walked in, their faces careful masks of neutrality. Only Gideon threw his old friend a quick grin as he sat down five chairs away from Velvet. Beside him, Eluard's hands twitched, apparently itching to draw a knife.

Not a bad one indeed, Jaghar concluded grimly, remembering Vander's words of the previous day. But if Velvet was right – if Aldred indeed maintained that crowning an unmarried woman was as unlawful as crowning a murderer...

Eluard himself wouldn't be enough. And yet that smile had looked vaguely satisfied. What in the world was she planning to do?

Before he could work up the courage to walk forward and simply ask her, Aldred was already standing and speaking.

Jaghar didn't hear much of his introduction, and remembered even less of it. While the old duke croaked on about a tragically lost life and the eminent importance of the Council's task at hand, his eyes made another round through the room – mostly ambassadors and inhabitants of the castle, but some more interesting faces as well. Rolland had faithfully shown up, and two rows behind the goldsmith he found Hamond – what in the world was *he* doing here? Perhaps Madelena knew, but Madelena was standing in the far back of the room amongst what looked like a clutter of messenger girls to the uninformed eye...

'... must start by disclosing a shocking discovery made by Lord Eluard and myself,' Aldred finished his monologue at the head of the hall.

Jaghar turned back to the table of dukes. His fingers drummed restlessly against his thigh, and he didn't seem able to stop them.

'Shall I?' Eluard said, standing up as well, and Aldred gestured him to go ahead.

The duke's report was short, clear, and shocking in the best sense of the word. Unpleasant details were recounted in full, with only a quick apology at the lady fainting in the third row; the utter lack of remorse was mentioned, as were Emeric's sneers at the address of his niece. By the time the young man finished speaking, Wymond had turned purple, and Laudine so pale that the line between her face and her white hair was hard to find. In the silence that fell at the end of Eluard's monologue, Jaghar could hear Gerald's nervous sniffling even from twenty feet away.

Then, breaking the shocked quiet of the hall with a single gruff chuckle, Gideon said, 'This is ridiculous.'

And all of a sudden everyone in the room was speaking, feverish whispers spreading from the front rows to the very back of the hall until only two quiet islands were left in the sea of shock and confusion. Velvet hadn't moved, hadn't even turned her head at the lady fainting behind her seat. Five chairs away from her, Emeric was gaping at the table before him, his puffy face so aghast that it would have been comical in any other context.

He didn't run, however. Did he realise he'd never pass the guards at the door, or had his reflexes abandoned him in the shock?

'Silence!' Aldred thundered, and within a heartbeat the hall was silent as death except for the echoes of the old duke's voice bouncing back from the ceiling.

'This is *ridiculous*,' Gideon repeated before anyone else could speak up. He was grinning an expectant grin, as if he had become the victim of some poorly executed joke and was waiting for someone to admit to the plot. 'Why in the world would Emeric kill his *brother*? Good gods, this whole story sounds like some Androughan clan feud, not like anything we civilised people—'

'It may not be so ridiculous as you believe it is, Gideon,' Laudine interrupted sharply. 'I did receive a letter from Reginald last night. My nephew, who—'

'Yes, yes, I heard – very tragic.'

'His letter was sent to my home first and had to be sent after me, so it arrived a little late – but it confirmed the rumours I already heard at Rock Hall. Trystan planned to appoint the princess as his heir.' A quick nod at Velvet. 'A decision he took the morning before he was killed, if I understand Reginald's letter correctly. One might imagine that upon hearing about this plan, the king's – brother...'

Her disgust at the last word was clearly audible, and Emeric jumped up without further pretences of politeness. 'Now listen here, for the gods' sake—'

'Would you sit down?' Wymond snapped at him. 'We're in the middle of a Council meeting, and I don't believe anyone asked *you* to speak.'

Gideon made a wide gesture at the other end of the table. 'You must allow the man to defend himself, at least.'

'Oh, I thought you had taken the defence on your shoulders already?'

Gideon uttered a joyless laugh. 'I'm not defending anyone, just saying I'd like to have a little more evidence before I jump to any conclusions. We can't call a man a murderer based on some wild report of an overheard conversation – for a start, you must admit it sounds ridiculously coincidental that he left his door open just for a couple of passing nobles to hear him blurt out a confession.'

'Not entirely coincidental,' Eluard said before Wymond could snap back another answer. 'We didn't accidentally walk past – we were alerted to the conversation by a passing servant. If you'd like to have more witnesses, I suppose we can ask him to tell us.'

'That's a *servant*!' Gideon rolled his eyes. 'And he didn't see the speaker either, did he? So all we know is that *someone*—'

'In Prince Emeric's personal rooms.'

'That *someone*, who may as well have broken into those rooms—'

'Speaking in Prince Emeric's voice.'

'And who we'll have to trust from your account sounded anywhere like the prince – yes, exactly.' Gideon snorted. 'It makes very little sense, Eluard, you'll have to admit that. Some heroic servant helping you? Some mysterious woman showing up *only* to—'

'I beg your pardon, my lord?' a voice from the public interrupted.

Jaghar jolted around. Rolland had risen to his feet, impressively square-shaped underneath his expensive shirt. The goldsmith was waving a sheet of parchment at shoulder-height, with an apologetic grimace.

'And who are you?' Aldred snapped.

'Rolland of the Squires' Quarter, my lord. Guild master of the goldsmiths' guild. Also...' His gaze trailed aside. Jaghar met his eyes, for hardly a single heartbeat – but long enough to see the bitter anger in the man's look. Whatever Rosin had told him, she clearly hadn't avoided his name.

Rolland abruptly turned back to Aldred and lifted his letter another inch. 'Also, my lord, this letter was given to me by the woman in question. She asked me to make sure you'd read it during the meeting of—'

'You know her?' Wymond cut in.

'I – eh – have formed a long-standing friendship with her, my lord.'

Eluard snorted a laugh. Laudine's face was an epitome of prim disapproval. Beside her, Aldred beckoned the goldsmith closer with a single gesture of his bony fingers.

'Give me that letter, then.'

Rolland trudged forward to hand the duke his letter, then turned back around with another venomous glare at Jaghar's direction. Jaghar raised an eyebrow. The smith wisely left the confrontation at that. Behind his broad back, Velvet was trembling, but she didn't look away from the parchment for a moment – demon be damned, he should somehow have made clear to her what had happened last night...

Aldred broke the wax with a snap that reverberated through the silent hall. It seemed that nobody even dared to breathe as he rolled out the letter.

'My lords, my lady,' he read – the greeting Rosin had put to paper herself. 'I hope you will forgive me for interrupting your Council meeting through this letter. My name is Rosaline, Rosin for the well-informed, and I have worked at Rock Hall for a number of years...'

Jaghar closed his eyes. Even read by Aldred's dry, croaking voice, he heard her behind the words, with that amused undertone of slight mockery. He knew the thoughts that had lived in her mind at the moment she wrote down these words. Even after that final push over the edge, they left him aching for vengeance.

'If this letter is delivered to you,' Aldred continued, with a slight pause, 'that means I'll have left town and will not return.'

Jaghar glanced over his shoulder. A frown was growing on Rolland's face – not what the goldsmith had expected to hear, presumably.

'Through my writing I want to apologise for the pain I have caused. I cooperated with Prince Emeric to kill his brother and Lord Reginald because I have been in love with him for years and believed he would make me his wife in return for my help. As it turned out, I was mistaken. The prince made clear, following these murders, that he would never love me. All I can do now to make up for my mistake is...'

'But this is *nonsense*!' Emeric shouted, jumping up again. 'I've never – this woman – she—'

'... to tell the court the truth of the king's death,' Aldred flatly continued. 'Prince Emeric killed his brother. I killed his secretary at his orders, because we believed Lord Reginald to be the only other person aware of the king's plan to appoint his daughter as his heir. This is all I have to say. You'll never see me again. Signed, Rosaline, daughter of—'

'Well,' Wymond said, leaning forward before Emeric could interrupt again, 'that seems crystal clear to me, wouldn't you say, Gideon?'

Jaghar glanced at Velvet. She was sitting with her hand clutched over her mouth – shock, one would say at first glance, but he vaguely suspected she might be hiding a grin.

'Guild master Rolland?' Eluard said, and in the audience the square man stood up again, looking dazed and a little nauseous.

'I – yes, my lord?'

'You said you know this woman personally.'

'I – good gods, my lord.' Rolland swallowed. 'I was unaware her letter contained anything of this nature – I believed – she suggested it was about someone else's crimes, not about – about—'

'Yes, yes,' Eluard interrupted him. 'But you know her? You can confirm that this woman named Rosaline exists, that she once worked at Rock Hall and that she gave you this sealed letter?'

Rolland nodded, stupefied. Eluard sighed as he leaned back in his chair.

'Then the case seems rather clear to me, truly.'

'But...' Emeric started again, by now paler than a sheet of snow. Wymond snorted loud enough to interrupt him, and even Gideon didn't object.

'Well,' Laudine said briskly. 'In that case, I don't suppose the Council should vote in favour of this, pardon me the wording, piece of excrement before us? Especially considering that Trystan himself was already planning to name the princess his heir instead?'

Jaghar realised, to his dismay, that he was holding his breath. He hardly seemed to be the only one in the unmoving silence that followed. Please. Please just say yes, please kick the bastard into the cells and never let him see the light of day again – please, *please* put that silk cloak around the shoulders where it belongs...

'Taking into consideration the duties of the Council,' Aldred said, 'I am not entirely sure that should be our conclusion.'

The air in his lungs escaped so abruptly that it hurt.

'Oh, *please*.' Eluard all but rolled his eyes. 'You cannot in all honesty maintain that crowning that bloody *murderer*—'

'As I told Lord Eluard already after our discovery of yesterday,' Aldred croaked, somehow loud enough to interrupt the younger duke, 'you are listening to your personal preferences speaking, not to the laws. It is the role of the Council to ensure the laws are followed when there is no king to do so. Therefore, we must look at what the laws tell us about this situation.'

'Yes!' Gerald piped up, speaking for the first time since the beginning of the meeting. 'I agree with Lord Aldred that this is the only reasonable approach in this matter!'

Jaghar nearly groaned. At the table Wymond and Laudine exchange a meaningful look – had Velvet told them about the young duke's marriage plans, or had his partiality become obvious already even in his single day at the castle?

'I read the relevant articles tonight,' Aldred continued as he laid out his sheets of parchment before him, utterly ignoring Gerald and his useless opinions. 'The interesting fact to take into account here is, I believe, that the king or queen of the Peaks cannot be charged with any criminal facts, including murder. Which raises the interesting question whether we can in any way penalise Prince Emeric – or perhaps I should say, King Emeric – for this deed. If he became the king the moment he committed the murder—'

'You cannot be serious!' Laudine interrupted, her voice an octave too high.

'If we look at the jurisprudence, there is unfortunately no earlier comparable case in the royal family – *however*...' Aldred gave Laudine a stern glance, just in case she'd interrupt him again. 'There are of course numerous examples of dukes, earls, and counts killing their fathers or brothers, and as far as I've been able to find, that never stops them from being named the next duke, earl, or count in line even if—'

'Dukes, earls, and counts don't get a Council when they die,' Wymond snapped, his long face reddening again. 'The entire bloody point is that Emeric isn't king yet – nobody is the king or queen at this moment – and as a mere prince he can be sent to the gallows as well as any other man.'

'That is *your* personal interpretation.'

'This is *madness*, Aldred!'

'Not as mad as crowning an unmarried girl without any—'

'Ah,' Velvet interrupted, and to Jaghar's bewilderment, she sounded calmly amused rather than on the brink of spitting fury. 'There appears to be some misunderstanding at play, Lord Aldred.'

Aldred swept around to face her so quickly that he shoved Gerald off his chair with his bony elbows, sending his wishful future son-in-law flailing into Eluard's arms.

'I beg your pardon?'

'You don't seem to be entirely aware of the latest developments,' Velvet informed him, still in that strange, cheerful tone that sent shivers of confusion up Jaghar's spine. What in the world was she *doing*? 'For which I obviously can't blame you, considering the way in which matters occurred. But the Council may want to know that I am, as a matter of fact, not an unmarried woman at the moment.'

At once the hall became quiet enough to hear the wind whisper along the walls outside. Jaghar stared at her, the hairs rising in the back of his neck. Not an unmarried woman? Had she spontaneously married the first duke at hand while he was busy shoving his aspiring fiancée off a cliff?

'You are – not?' Aldred repeated.

Velvet stood up and threw a glance over her shoulder. 'Hamond?'

The High Priest pulled a roll of parchment from a bag at his feet and walked to the head of the hall. Somehow, Jaghar noted, nervousness itching in his guts, the man looked less confident than usual. Velvet, what in the world...

Aldred snatched the parchment from the High Priest's hands and unrolled it with the full Council unceremoniously leaning over his shoulders to read along. For a fraction of an instant nothing moved in the hall but the seven pairs of eyes shooting along the writing.

Jaghar averted his face for a moment, took a deep breath to calm his hammering heart, and looked up again.

And then those same seven pairs of eyes were staring in his direction.

CHAPTER 19

'W hat in hell?' Aldred broke the silence, his voice growing explosively louder in those few short syllables.

Viviette smiled at him. She couldn't stop smiling. Was it Emeric's terrified expression? The dumbfounded bewilderment in Aldred's eyes? Or the beginning of the broadest of grins on Wymond's face? Whatever the reason, the corners of her mouth refused to be discouraged in the slightest despite her best attempts to look at least a *little* regal about the lies she was about to feed the world.

'I believe the contract is clear, Lord Aldred?'

"*Clear*?' the duke burst out. 'Do you call this *clear*? Are we supposed to think – do you want us to accept – when did this—'

'Can anybody tell me,' Emeric interrupted shrilly, 'what the damn thing is saying?'

A short, dead silence fell. Then Wymond chuckled and said, 'He married her to the Spymaster.'

'He did *what*?'

The audience behind her burst out in shocked gasps and cries of surprise, drowning out even the answer Aldred was trying to give. Now finally Viviette dared to glance in Jaghar's direction. She had watched him from the corner of her eye from the moment he appeared – a reassuring figure in black and silver even hidden in the shadows – but he had been too late for her to tell him anything, to warn him, to prepare him for the role she needed him to play...

His gaze met hers for only the shortest fraction of a moment. In that tiny moment she could see the landslide of his thoughts shove by on his face – from confusion to that sharp, simple focus that had kept him alive for all these years, a focus of survival, of shoving all questions aside until the war was over. A cool curtain seemed to draw by behind his dark eyes. The moment he looked away from her, he was again the Spymaster who had both scared and infuriated her for years of her life –

'You seem rather surprised?' he said, and if she hadn't known better, Viviette wouldn't have been able to tell he was no less astonished himself.

'What in the world…' Aldred started.

At the same moment, Emeric jumped up and ran.

Viviette's cry to stop him never made it to her lips. Around her uncle's path to the only exit people jumped up and dove forward to contain him; within moments, Sir Bertram emerged from the clew of limbs and furious shouts with Emeric's wrists tightly clutched in his fists and a bitter grimace on his weathered face. Despite Aldred's furious commands behind her, the knight met Viviette's eyes first.

'Don't worry, Your Highness – Your Majesty?' He shrugged, giving Emeric's arm another yank as her uncle tried to wrench out of his grip. 'The rat isn't going anywhere.'

'Very grateful, Bertram. Would you—'

'Now listen a moment,' Aldred snapped. 'We have not even confirmed yet that she – that the princess is indeed…'

'This marriage certificate *does* seem quite convincing to me,' Wymond said dryly. 'The High Priest himself affirmed it – and this definitely *is* Trystan's seal.'

'Yes, yes, but who in hell is the other witness – what's the name, Madelena?'

'Ah, yes.' Madelena's voice rose from the back of the hall without a trace of hesitation, and for a moment Viviette was so relieved she thought she might faint. 'That's me. The king asked me to be a witness. Was honoured to do so, of course.'

Aldred squinted at her. 'And you are?'

'Your new Spymaster, as it happens to be,' Jaghar said, and Aldred narrowed his eyes even further.

'I've never even seen her before.'

'That's correct. She's rather good at the job.'

A few people sniggered in the audience, quite to their own surprise, it seemed; at the table of the Council, Wymond laughed out loud. Viviette slowly breathed out. Her father's old friend was the only one among them who should know something strange was going on – a marriage contract appearing two days after she had spoken with him, and not mentioned anything like a marriage at all? But he appeared quite content to forget about that small issue, and around him, none of the other dukes shared Aldred's suspicious scowl.

'Well,' Wymond said, falling back in his chair with his grin still lingering on his face. 'Good old Trystan. Never a boring day. Care to explain the whole story, Vivi?'

'Happily.' She gave him a thin smile. 'Father knew he was in danger. He knew the danger might be coming from – well, within the family. He wanted me to marry, and marry fast – that was the plan to make sure I would indeed be his heir, which Reginald wrote about. After the mess we found at the Floating Castle, he wanted to be sure my husband would at least be someone he could trust. The rest, I believe, is quite clear.'

'And then he didn't tell a single person about it?' Aldred snapped. 'And neither did you? No celebration? No—'

'As you may have noticed,' Jaghar cut in, sounding nearly bored, 'some murderer was willing to kill his brother for the throne. After Trystan's death, it seemed wiser not to spread the news that his niece should be his next target.'

'Strange as the notion may seem to you,' Viviette added, 'I prioritise my heartbeat over wedding cakes. We'll have the celebration later.'

She felt Jaghar's eyes on her and didn't dare to turn for fear she might burst out crying, or laughing, or both, in full view of the court. Under her persistent stare, Aldred seemed to shrink by the heartbeat.

'But he can't – in all honesty – have wanted us to crown some – some...'

'Yes?' Viviette said sharply, but before he could find some less affronting alternative to the words on his tongue, Jaghar spoke up on the other side of the hall.

'I'm afraid you are listening to your personal preferences speaking here, Lord Aldred, not to the laws. Perhaps, considering the duty of the Council...'

Now Wymond was not the only one laughing; Laudine, at least, was suspiciously quick to cover her mouth with a gloved hand, and Eluard averted his face with shaking shoulders.

'Apart from that point,' Jaghar continued, a hint of coldness sneaking back into his voice, 'I'd strongly discourage you from trying to crown anyone but the princess. She is the king's intended heir. Keep the cloak away from me, if you will.'

Viviette closed her eyes. Pure sunshine was melting through her, warming even the most distant tips of her fingers.

'Well,' Wymond broke the silence, sounding like he was still grinning. 'In that case, shall we cast our votes? I believe we should be done discussing by now. At least I can tell you already that following her father's explicit wishes, I vote in favour of Princess Viviette to take the throne of the Peaks.'

'And so do I,' Laudine said.

Viviette opened her eyes. Next to Laudine, Osric was staring at her, his thoughts visibly running on high speed behind his eyes – he had no idea of her opinions on diamond smuggle, she might not be as mild as Emeric – but then again, if he voted against her and she still won, how mild would that make her?

He swallowed. 'And so do I.' His voice came out hoarse, but clear.

All eyes rested on Aldred now. The old duke looked up from the parchment still in his hands, glared at Jaghar, then at her, then back at the parchment. He gave the impression he had to force the words over his lips – 'And so do I.'

'Obviously,' Gerald immediately said, 'so do I, too, considering—'

'And so do I,' Eluard interrupted, silencing him at once.

At the far end of the row, Gideon sat slumped back in his chair, drops of sweat pearling over his forehead. He opened his mouth, shut it again, glanced at Emeric's sagged figure in Bertram's unyielding arms, then looked back up at Viviette. Something seemed to fall down in his eyes as their gazes met.

'And so do I,' he said.

And all her mind was able to contain was Wymond's triumphant voice – 'All hail the queen...'

She found herself back in front of the throne without a recollection of how she had walked there, or when, or why. The world came to her in loose fragments, shattered observations and shreds of sounds. Wymond's hands on her shoulders. Eluard's bright voice, congratulating her three times in a row. The heavy, floral fragrance of Laudine's perfume and the sharp tang of Aldred's sweat. Her uncle's furious shouts, dying away in the distance as her knights dragged him out of the hall.

And then the cold weight of the gold on her head. The light, slippery silk on her shoulders, and Laudine's gentle hands buttoning it shut on her chest.

Three days to prepare – a lifetime to prepare – and yet it was happening far too fast for her senses. It seemed to her she was looking down at herself from the ceiling of the hall, standing pale and frozen before the court, smiling mechanically for reasons she could hardly recall herself. People swarmed around her, yelling about banners and decorations, pressing her hands with congratulating remarks she barely heard, inquiring about dresses and celebratory dinners as if she had any opinions on veal and fruit cakes *now*...

Then the world went quiet.

Viviette slammed back into her own mind, back behind her own eyes. Around her, the crowd hastily shuffled away, their smiles paling, their gazes pointed at something approaching behind her back. When she whirled around, Jaghar's glare was just persuading a last nobleman to take a lightning-quick step back – and then few more steps, too. By the time he reached her, an empty circle had spread out around them, dozens of eyes following his every moment from a safe distance.

And yet he didn't stop moving, didn't stand still at the usual two-foot distance. He wrapped his slender fingers around her upper arms and pulled her closer, the strength of his touch warm against her skin even through her velvet sleeves – a touch that allowed no objection, no hesitation, nothing but simple, immediate surrender. Viviette followed his unspoken demand as by reflex, stepping closer until he stood so near that he might have kissed her by simply bowing his head. Barely three inches separating their bodies. The dangerous warmth on her arms. The laughter lines around his eyes, the smile trembling around the corners of his lips – and only then, at seeing the quiet triumph on his face, did she dare to believe what she had done, what she had managed –

The silk cloak was hers.

He was hers.

Vaguely, in a faraway part of her mind, she was still aware of the dozens of eyes following their every movement, the onlookers hungry for gossip or political leverage... But the rest of the world seemed utterly unreal to her, an infinite sea of nothingness around the island only the two of them inhabited.

'Did I tell you,' he murmured, so quietly that no one would be able to hear them even in the silence surrounding them, 'that you're still absolutely, utterly insane?'

Her smile seemed to originate somewhere in the deepest core of her chest, branching through her in sprouts of warm, golden happiness. The corners of her mouth perked up as by their own will.

'I think you mentioned such a thing once or—'

'Hell be damned, Velvet.' He shook his head without taking his gaze off her, an unmistakable twinkle in his eyes. 'Or am I supposed to call you Your Majesty by now?'

'You do realise that makes you—'

'Shush, you,' he muttered, less and less successful at supressing his smile. 'Allow me to postpone thinking about that part for a few hours. I didn't go into this morning expecting to be a married man by lunchtime, let alone...'

'I'd have told you if you hadn't been so busy forging letters all night.'

'You're going to berate *me* for forging anything?'

A laugh – a full, uncontrollable laugh – welled up in her like the rising tide, nearly pressing her heart through her chest. Her gaze locked onto his eyes. A darkness to drown in, to sweep her off her feet and make her forget the world even existed...

'Kiss me, Velvet,' he said softly.

Her heart slammed into her throat. Suddenly she was sharply aware of the circle around them again, the eyes pricking into her skin from every direction – suddenly she could *hear* the thoughts running through those curious minds, the whispers that would be exchanged within minutes, the excited letters that would soon find their way to the most remote corners of the world...

'They're *looking,'* she whispered.

There was no denying the wicked smile around his lips now. 'And then what?'

'Oh, gods.' The pressure of his fingers on her skin was both dangerously tempting and temptingly dangerous. 'But – oh, gods, they'll *know.'*

'You just shoved a marriage certificate under their noses, Velvet. I think they know.'

'But...'

His right hand released her arm and ended up under her chin, tender fingers forcing her to look up at him. Far away, hardly audible over the rush of hot blood in her ears, a gasp or two rose from their audience.

'Besides,' he whispered, barely moving his lips, 'you're the queen. What are they going to do, kick you out of the castle?'

She parted her lips to object, then stayed silent as her mind failed to find the words. Good gods, what was she supposed to say? But imagine someone takes offense.

Imagine someone figures out what happened in the past months, imagine they tear that cloak off me and decide they might better crown Emeric anyway...

'But since that doesn't seem to convince you...' His smile broadened to devilish proportions. 'I suppose I might as well make it an order.'

'An—'

'I'm quite sure that's one of those things I'm allowed to do now, Velvet.'

Again she almost laughed out loud, a tingling desire spreading from his fingertips against her skin through the rest of her body. The mischievous gleam in his eyes. The challenge in his smile. An order – gods be damned, this was a development she could get used to.

'I see,' she whispered, closing her eyes. 'In that case...'

And then there was nothing but his kiss, erasing the eyes of the court, erasing the sleepless nights, erasing the doubts and fears and sorrows of the world until his promise of happiness came seeping into the very marrow of her bones.

EPILOGUE

'So,' Velvet said in a hushed tone, standing at his arm in her impressive creation of light-blue silk, lace and pearls. Around her even the dark Temple room looked sunny, its dusty smell washed out by her fragrance of blossoming spring flowers, its usual silence broken by the soft murmur of the guests gathered two doorways away. 'Quick question – do you think Tamar might have plans with Lord Everild?'

'Fascinating idea,' Jaghar said, unable to suppress a grin. 'Would expect her to have better taste, I must admit, but who knows. What made you think?'

Madelena said he suddenly cancelled the service for tonight. Also, Tamar has been rowing with Amiran, so he won't be around her rooms tonight – and you have to admit she was unusually friendly with Everild yesterday. '

'You mean she didn't seem about to behead him?'

Velvet gave him a broad grin from behind her delicate veil. 'Well, exactly.'

'Could be,' Jaghar admitted, nodding slowly. 'Interesting. Lends more credibility to Madelena's idea that she's been having... meetings with some other noblemen back home.'

'Yes, I thought about that too. Although none of them seems to be particularly successful so far.'

'I may hope she puts the bar a little higher if she marries again,' Jaghar said dryly. 'But it's a damn pity she is getting in the service's way – I was quite looking forward to Everild's opinion on those iffy family finances after the old man's death.'

'Still wondering if they didn't just kill him. It really *was* a very convenient—'

'Good gods, Vivi,' Wymond's voice interrupted her from behind, sounding undeniably amused. 'Do the two of you ever *stop*?'

Velvet whirled around, with her most innocent look on her face. 'Oh, hello Wymond! Didn't hear you coming. Beautiful weather for a wedding day, isn't it?'

The duke laughed out loud. 'Beautiful day to at least speak about something else than murders for once, I'd say.'

'Ah, yes,' Jaghar said, with a quick grin. 'Apologies. You look lovely, Your Majesty. Nice dress, did I tell you?'

He had told her that morning, in fact, to which she'd replied she couldn't wait for him to tear it off her again. The tremble around the corners of her mouth told him he wasn't the only one who remembered the exchange.

'Thanks,' she said, looking away just before he burst out laughing. 'You look pretty intimidating too. Goes well with your most murderous expression, I think.'

'Lovely. I'll try to look a little dangerous, that will give our guests something to gossip about.'

'Very courteous,' Velvet said brightly. 'They've travelled a long way, they deserve at least some scandalous whispering. Are they all seated, Wymond? If I'm only allowed to talk about dresses, we might as well get started.'

The duke chuckled. 'They are. I came to see if you were ready. Which I suppose you are?'

'Of course.'

'Wonderful. I'll do my bit, then.'

And he was off again. In the other room the voices hushed as he entered, and it was in that sudden, heavy silence that the tension unexpectedly set its claws in Jaghar's heart.

This was happening.

All of this was really, truly happening.

It shouldn't have caught him so violently after a full winter to get used to the sight of his signature on that marriage contract. But he had still never spoken his vows. He had still used a separate bedroom – Emeric's bedroom, because sometimes pettiness was simply the most pleasant option. And of course he had slipped into

Velvet's bed nearly every night, had eaten his meals by her side, had whispered the words of that sacred vow in her ears while she was sleeping, just to know how they felt on his lips –

But now he was standing here, in a quiet Temple room, with the world's most brilliant woman on his arm, and all of it seemed to carry more meaning than his poor mortal mind could comprehend.

'Jaghar?' Velvet whispered next to him.

He turned to meet her eyes, wide and bright green behind her veil. The light amusement had vanished from her expression too, and her hand tensed on his arm.

'Hm?'

'It's just – so strange he isn't here.'

For a moment his mind failed to come up with a single sensible thought – just cold, blank emptiness, accompanied by that muffled sting that had replaced the worst of the grief as the months went by. Two rooms away, he heard Wymond's voice welcoming the honoured guests and informing them without further explanation that he, rather than the High Priest himself, would lead the ceremony of this morning.

'Yes,' he said quietly.

Wordlessly, she leaned over to hug him, careful not to wrinkle her dress. He wrapped an arm around her and pressed a kiss against her temple, just beside the veil.

'Then again,' she whispered, 'you are here.'

He smiled, even though it took a little effort. 'Not going anywhere either.'

She moved back again, her hand remaining around his waist. Wymond's voice continued in the background – 'We have gathered in this Temple today to celebrate the union between Queen Viviette of the Peaks and her husband...'

Her smile broke through at that last word, so bright that Jaghar nearly laughed out loud – a smile that somehow washed all hurts and painful memories from his mind like sunlight melting the snow away. At the sight of it, it took all of his self-restraint not to tear away her veil and kiss her senseless before they set a single step into the altar room itself.

'Well,' she said, reaching him a hand. 'Husband?'

His heart leapt in his chest. 'Wife?'

She smiled even broader. 'It's about time we go face them, isn't it?'

'Yes,' Jaghar said, drawing in a deep breath as he took her soft hand in his. 'It's high, high time.'

The day passed in a blur of loose impressions, each more bewildering than the last. The trumpets blaring the melody that announced the king's arrival as their open coach drove onto Rock Hall's courtyard again. An abundance of bows and curtsies, as though suddenly nobody could keep standing around him. Tamar, who greeted him with an amused 'Colleague' when she found him in the banquet hall to congratulate him.

'That,' Jaghar said, 'is possibly the most ridiculous thing anyone has said to me all winter.'

Velvet giggled out loud by his side – like she laughed at everything for the rest of the afternoon as she whirled through the room and greeted friends and fellow nobles and foreign diplomats. He heard every silvery laugh, every excited exclamation, even from half a hall away. It was that sound that imprinted itself upon his memory, rather than the endless felicitations from nervous-looking guests who still seemed prepared for the possibility he'd respond by listing all their most shameful secrets out loud in public.

He did no such thing, although he was tempted when an exceptionally sweaty Riverlands ambassador showed up to pass on Donovan's wishes. No good wishes. Simply wishes. But causing half a war at a wedding would perhaps spoil Velvet's mood, so Jaghar restrained himself and told the diplomat to tell his king that the wishes had been received with an appropriate amount of appreciation.

Velvet's eyes were twinkling when she found him minutes later, wrapped her fingers around his elbow, and muttered, 'I understand you're appropriately enjoying yourself, husband?'

He laughed as his heart made another leap. 'Is Madelena spying on me for you now?'

'Not even, this time,' she said, her smile broadening. 'Eluard heard you. Think he still hasn't stopped laughing. But perhaps we should ask Madelena to keep an eye on—'

'Already did this morning.'

'Of *course* you already did.'

He grinned. 'Apologies. Hard to avoid some duplicate ideas with three Spymasters at Rock Hall.'

'I'm appropriately amused at this remark,' Velvet said cheerfully, then dashed away to go speak with Lady Zovinar of Tanglewood and her broad-shouldered husband on the other side of the hall. Jaghar found himself grinning after her like an idiot, and couldn't even care much.

They were reunited at dinner, seated in customary isolation at the head of the main table, so that even the other royal guests sat at least six feet away from them. Quite an annoying tradition, Jaghar had found at previous noble weddings in Rock Hall – it made it nearly impossible to hear what newlywed targets were discussing over their meal. Tonight he was grateful enough to make up for all those earlier evenings of irritation. Of course the looking eyes were still there, curious and concerned, but it was the first time since the ceremony they were even allowed a private word for longer than a few moments.

The first time since the ceremony she was this close to him, too, her leg brushing past his every other heartbeat, their elbows meeting with every turn. The first time he allowed himself to realise that this day would eventually be over – that they would escape this crowded hall sooner or later, that a royal bedroom was waiting for them upstairs...

'You just know they're all thinking the same thing, don't you,' Velvet said, reading his mind as usual even with her twinkling eyes scanning the hall. 'They're not even *trying* to be subtle about staring.'

He laughed, a sting of arousal curling through his guts. 'I think they're a little concerned for you, generally speaking.'

'And you're not even looking *that* frightening today.'

'Won't suddenly make them forget the tales they've heard about the things these Androughan savages do with their women. Imagine the horror, an innocent young lady like you forced to hand herself over to the whims of some brute like me...'

Her slender hand lowered to his thigh and lingered there for the shortest moment. 'Oh, yes, my poor virginal heart. I forgot about that for a moment.'

'Can assure you all the old ladies giving you concerned glances didn't forget,' he said dryly. 'It's a surprise nobody fainted yet.'

'It's a surprise I didn't faint yet, hearing you summing it up like that. Do you think they'd let us leave earlier if I did?'

His grin broke through. 'Yes, but you'd probably be surrounded by an army of maids until long after sunset. Not sure if that's what you're aiming for.'

'A shame.' Another deep sigh, followed by an impressively innocent glance in his direction, with wide green eyes and her lips set in a helpless pout. 'I'll just look chaste and virtuous for another few hours then. The sacrifices I have to bring...'

Jaghar closed his eyes for a moment, battling his laughter as much as his arousal. In that cloud of light-blue silk, with a slight blush on her dainty face and a pained gleam in her eyes, she succeeded unnervingly well at imitating the timid, unsuspecting young lady she was supposed to be – and somehow that contrast, the thought of how thoroughly he'd spoil that innocence in mere hours, was enough to turn him to steel despite his best attempts to control himself.

'If you're trying to discourage me, I'm afraid you're failing hopelessly, Velvet.'

She lowered her eyes with another sigh as she turned back to her plate and shook her head, looking even more innocent. 'A cruel man you are, indeed.'

He was, as a matter of fact, quite in the mood for cruelty by the time the many dinner courses were finally behind them, all speeches were given, and all gifts had been presented. Perhaps a few carefully applied injuries would at least make these people understand that he didn't care much about his five new horses of the finest breed, not if he could also spend the time peeling a wedding dress off his wife...

His *wife*. He still had to pinch himself to believe it.

But finally the festivities came to an end, and finally the first guests withdrew to their bedrooms. Still an annoying number of them stayed around, glancing at the main table too frequently to pretend the wine was the primary reason – but by this point Jaghar was quite done caring what the court would think of him if they didn't stay until the very last guest had gone. If he was the king of this place now – another pinch-worthy thought – he might as well do what he wanted every now and then.

'Velvet?'

She turned away from the table to their left, where Gerald was stubbornly yet unsuccessfully trying to engage Aldred's daughter in a chat. 'Hm?'

'Imagine I just picked you up and carried you out of here – would you have any substantial objections to that idea?'

'Apart from you having waited this long to come up with it, not at all.'

Jaghar laughed, got to his feet, and lifted her from her chair in a single movement, finding the soft contours of her body underneath the masses of lace and slippery silk. Around them the persistent rumble of voices faltered for a heartbeat, then continued suspiciously eagerly. But Velvet giggled against his chest, and he really didn't feel like listening to anyone or anything else tonight.

'Wymond?' he said, looking up as he turned towards the exit. 'We're off. Are you taking care of the rest?'

The duke jovially lifted his glass. 'I'll make sure the wine gets finished, don't worry.'

Jaghar grinned. 'Knew we could count on you.'

He felt the stares stinging after them as he made his way to the door, heard the whispers rising in his wake –

but with Velvet's tempting weight pressed against his chest, the flowery scent of her perfume surrounding him, not even his usual invisibility seemed of any importance to him anymore. Let them stare, let them see him for once. They might as well find out he was a human being after all.

Memories rose in him as he made his way through the silent castle, up the stairs and through the high, dark corridors he knew well enough to navigate them with his eyes closed – memories of the first time he had set foot in Rock Hall, the walls whispering secrets at him from every corner, waiting to be heard... The languages he hadn't known, the unfamiliar faces. The frightful rumours behind his back, and the nosy little girl glowering at him from under her dark curls whenever he stumbled over her –

He looked down. She lay against his chest with her eyes closed, her face radiating such pure, drowsy happiness that he nearly lowered her to her feet to kiss her heart out on this very staircase, damn the passing nobles and servants.

His, finally.

Like it was all his now – the shadows of Rock Hall and the majestic mountains outside, this land that had welcomed him as a dead man and turned him back to life... His. A realisation that would perhaps never truly get through to him, but then again –

Velvet looked up to meet his gaze when he reached the door of the royal bedroom, and at the sight of the gleam in her eyes, he'd have believed they'd secretly crowned him emperor of the entire known world in the meantime.

A small smile crept up on her lips in that infinitesimal moment he stood there, unmoving, half a step removed from the bedroom they would share for the rest of their lives. It was a smile that carried both memories and expectations, challenges and reassurances. I'm here, that smile said. I'll never be anywhere else again.

Jaghar pushed open the door and lifted her to kiss her in the same movement. They dashed into the candle-lit room in a flutter of silk and breathless excitement, their lips locked, their bodies entwined; he barely had the time to kick the door shut behind him before her hands found their way under the dark velvet of his clothes. They half fell, half crashed into the furs and blankets, ruining the careful patterns of flower petals that someone had placed there. Velvet yanked open his coat with impatient hands and grabbed at his shirt, laughing and moaning under his kiss. She was gasping for breath when he pulled away and came up on his knees to look down on her. Framed by ruffled blue silk and messy dark curls, eyeing him with indisputable desire, she seemed another woman entirely than the innocent young queen who had sat beside him at the dinner table.

'I've seen you looking more virginal, Velvet.'

'I'm well aware you have,' she muttered, a small grin on her face. 'You didn't seem unhappy with the experience.'

He chuckled and slipped his fingers underneath her skirt, brushing over the satin skin of her ankle. Velvet closed her eyes, her breath quickening. Under his fingertips, the muscles of her lower leg tensed at every touch as he made his way up, inch by inch, circling over the impossible softness of her body with leisurely, nearly dreamlike slowness. Her hands clenched to fists in the silk of her wedding dress. Her lips parted a fraction in a moan that was yet to emerge. So much time had gone by since that first night, so much had happened in the meantime – and yet he still found traces of that same astonished delight in her expression, as if she'd never stopped being astounded at all she could feel.

Her thighs parted as by command when he passed her knees, but he lingered there, his fingers pressed against the soft inside of her legs as he bent over to kiss her. She received him with hot, hungry lips, wrapping her hands around the back of his neck to pull him closer. Their tongues twisted together in a dance that tasted of honeyed fruit and bubbly dessert wine, promising the warmth of her body, a softness he would kill for.

Not unhappy with the experience...

'I've always been yours since that day,' he muttered, his lips still brushing hers. 'I may have needed some time to admit it – some more time to stop being afraid of it – but I've truly never wanted anything or anyone else since you showed up into my room and started ordering me around. You know that, don't you?'

'Jaghar—'

He smiled. 'Tell me.'

'You can't possibly know how grateful I am that I found you that night.' She barely breathed the words. 'How grateful I am that I could trust you. How happy you make me. How proud I am for everything you've battled and defeated – how much you deserve every single thing I can give you – and...'

She hesitated for the shortest moment. Jaghar bent over to press a kiss in the hollow of her neck, the weight of her words unfurling in his heart with a faint, tingling warmth. For possibly the first time in his life, he felt not the slightest urge to object.

'And?'

A smile curled around her lips, mischievous and staggeringly earnest at the same time. 'How honoured I am to be here with you – Your Majesty.'

Jaghar froze only for the shortest moment, then grabbed her around the waist and turned to his back in the same movement, so that she ended up lying on top of him. '*What* did you call me?'

'Your Majesty?' She giggled as he ripped open the lacing of her wedding dress, an elated, satisfied giggle that suggested she had been waiting for this occasion for far too long. 'I'm just—'

He came up and kissed the words off her lips as he yanked the silk off her, baring her slender shoulders and breasts. She dug her hands into his torso, fingers clawing into his muscles with delightful force. They tumbled around in the blankets again, a tangle of limbs and hot, demanding kisses; with a groan he pulled down the last of her dress. Your Majesty. *Your Majesty.* To hear it from *her* lips...

She broke their kiss, laughing. 'I'm just stating the facts, you see.'

He managed a laugh. 'I think you'll have to state the facts a few more times for me to get used to them.'

'Nothing I'd rather do, Your Majesty.'

'Nothing?'

'You sound like you're trying to prove me wrong on some – *oh...*'

Jaghar chuckled and slipped his finger along the soft wetness between her legs again, lingering for a moment at the spot where her lips met. Another gasp escaped her, and this one sounded like a surrender.

'Nothing?' he repeated softly.

'Alright, perhaps there are one or two things I'd rather – oh gods, *Jaghar*—'

'Perhaps, you say?' He leaned over her, slowly pressing two fingers into her at once, stretching her silken tightness around him. She arched closer, and he clutched his free hand in the small of her back to pin her slender body against his chest. 'Am I leaving any room for doubt?'

She moaned when he pulled out of her again, her legs clenching around his wrist as if to lock him in. 'Less and less, I must admit.' Her voice was a dazed whisper.

'Still too much for my taste, Velvet.'

'Then better make some effort to convince me, Your Majesty.'

'Oh,' he muttered, trailing his fingertips down along the inside of her thigh, 'you want an *effort*?'

Without waiting for her answer he bent his head and kissed the ridge of her collarbone. A shiver ran through her under his lips. Slowly he trailed further down her body, brushed a kiss on the marble skin of her breast, then closed his lips around her nipple and gently pinned it between his teeth. Her sharp hiss sent a flare of fierce hunger bursting through him – hell's sake, he wanted to yank open his trousers and take her, wanted to drown himself in the sweet warmth of her body until every single fibre of him understood she'd be his until his dying day...

But he'd have the rest of his life to convince himself of that fact, and this was not a night he wanted to be over any time soon.

Somehow he restrained himself, wandering further down her body with agonising slowness despite the raging erection threatening to burst from his underwear. Quiet moans rose from her lips when he finally reached the dark curls between her thighs and moved down the last inches, sucking and circling over her warm flesh and inhaling the salty scent and taste of her arousal. He knew the way her legs tensed around his shoulders as he teased her closer to a climax, knew the way her moans grew into hoarse cries, knew the way her fingers cramped in his hair to press him into that most sensitive spot between her lips –

And he knew when to stop, just when she sucked in that last sharp breath, just when her entire body arched into his caresses. She blurted out a curse when he pulled away from her, her voice hazy with lust.

'Jaghar...'

He chuckled. 'Shouldn't that be Your Majesty for you?'

'So cruel, indeed,' she muttered, her pained groan nearly convincing. 'What's an innocent woman to do in the face of such torture?'

'I'm quite sure you'll come up with something,' he said, and laid a fingertip against her entrance. She twitched around his touch, her muscles contracting in uncontrolled spasms. 'Or else I'll probably amuse myself for some time.'

'You – oh, gods...' Her laugh came suspiciously close to a cry of despair. 'You're going to make me beg for this, aren't you?'

'You could start by asking me politely,' he suggested dryly, unbuttoning his trousers with his free hand as he slowly ran a fingertip along the lines of her glistening lips. His erection emerged so hungry it nearly hurt. 'I understand politeness is your new favourite pastime?'

She twitched again as his finger passed a sensitive spot, half laughing, half moaning. 'Would you please – *Jaghar*! – oh gods, would you please just fuck me already?'

He raised an eyebrow, unable to suppress a smile. Her body throbbed under his touch – so, so close to release...

'Still feel like I'm missing something, Velvet.'

'Your – Majesty,' she groaned, biting her lip in an unsuccessful attempt to keep her grin down. He laughed and slipped his finger into her a last time, then came up to position himself between her thighs and laid his straining tip against her. She clawed her fingers into his buttocks to pull him closer, moaning when he didn't give way.

'Think I'm slowly getting used to this,' he whispered, and only then did he sink into her.

Her body closed tightly around him, still twitching in the rhythm of her arousal. Deeper and deeper did he delve into her, slowly until he could no longer restrain himself and thrust his last inch into her with sudden urgency, burying himself in her clenching warmth entirely. She gave in, then, tightened like a fist around him as she came in a convulsion of breathtaking pleasure, writhing against him and moaning his name. He wrapped his arms around her and held her against his chest until the waves subsided and only the shivers of her laughter still ran through her. 'Hell's sake, Jaghar...'

He carefully lowered her back into the blankets, still buried deep inside her, and kissed her feverish forehead. 'Don't think I've ever managed that before.'

She uttered a dazed laugh. 'Imagine – all the Copper Coast girls insisted life would get boring in the bedroom after marriage.'

'Oh, I have some unfortunate news for you.' He slowly ran his hand along her neck, her shoulder, the slender lines of her back. 'It doesn't work that way when you're unlucky enough marry some Androughan savage, you see. 'You'll have to wait with the boredom until I'm done amusing myself, I'm afraid...'

She shivered under his touch, a smile perking up around her lips. 'Good gods. Then at least I hope you have no scandalous amusement in mind, husband?'

'I must disappoint you again.' He slid half out of her, then thrust into her tightness again. Again she shivered. 'I want you in every single room of this castle – I want you in the garden, and on a mountain top too. I want you in public without the world noticing. I want you blindfolded and bound to this bed, I want to share you with another man, I want to make you come ten times in a row, and by the time we've finished that list...' He smiled. 'Well, perhaps we'll have time for boring.'

'What a daunting prospect,' she muttered, lying below him in the pillows with a drowsy smile on her face. 'But of course, if this is what my king and husband wants from me...'

Again he thrust into her, and her sentence evaporated on her lips, leaving only a hoarse moan behind. The last of his self-restraint crumbled. Clenching his fists into the blankets, he groaned, 'Want to know exactly what your king and husband wants from you, Velvet?'

A rosy giggle. 'Oh, please show me.'

He pushed into her without further warning, driving himself home into the warmth of her body. The fire of his hunger burst through him in all-consuming flares, wiped out all thoughts and sensations but the tightness of her grip on him, the dizzying need for release, the moans rising from her lips as he fucked her entangled in the messy blankets of their bed – *their* bed...

He came in a grunting eruption of ecstasy, melting into her as the waves of his climax crashed through him. Velvet clutched her arms around him, and he rolled to his side with their bodies still joined, holding her close until the last shivers of his release waned. There they lay in light-headed silence for minutes, her head on his shoulder and his face buried in her messy dark locks, while his heartbeat settled down to its usual rhythm and her fingers played along the scars on his chest with slow, feathery touches.

Finally, she mumbled, 'Getting used to the facts already, Your Majesty?'

Jaghar chuckled, moving his head to look her in the eyes. 'Try me, I'd say.'

'King Jaghar of the Peaks?'

He didn't flinch. 'Queen Viviette?'

'Pretty good,' she admitted brightly, moving up to kiss him. 'Husband?'

'Wife?'

She grazed her lips over his, so soft he barely felt the touch. For a heartbeat she hesitated, her forehead against his cheek, her breath stroking his neck and collarbone. Then, with only the smallest trace of a question in her voice, she whispered, 'Mine?'

Jaghar folded his arms closer around her and pressed her to his chest. Around them the fragrance of spring flowers mingled with the scent of her arousal; her soft, slow breathing was all that broke the silence of the room, all that moved in the stillness of his thoughts. Soon he'd kiss her again. Soon he'd touch every inch of her again, make love to her again, turn her mind inside out again...

But not yet. Not now.

'Mine,' he mumbled.

In this quiet moment – he was only stating the facts.

The End

OTHER BOOKS BY LISETTE MARSHALL

Are you looking for even more masks, murders and mysteries? The **free** novella *Damask* takes place between *Velvet* and *Leather*. It features Viviette and Jaghar as they try to solve an explosive case, and introduces Queen Tamar of Redwood, the heroine of a later trilogy.

You can get a copy of *Damask* by signing up for my newsletter at <u>www.lisettemarshall.com/damask</u>.

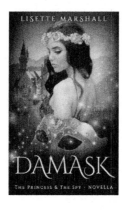

The Queen & The Assassin

**He was supposed to kill her, not to melt her iron
heart...**

When a common enemy threatens both their lives, a
ruthless queen and the assassin out for her life have
no choice but to close an uncertain alliance. And as
shadows of the past draw them deeper and deeper into
a tangle of deceit, sizzling hate turns into something
much more dangerous...

Court of Blood and Bindings

"They call him the Silent Death, because he kills without a sound and leaves none capable of speaking in his wake..."

When the empire's deadliest fae murderer catches her wielding forbidden magic, twenty-year-old Emelin believes her hour has come. Instead, he offers her a dangerous bargain.

Court of Blood and Bindings is the first book in the Fae Isles series, an epic fantasy romance featuring winged fae, powerful colour magic and passionate enemies to lovers romance.

ABOUT THE AUTHOR

Lisette Marshall is a fantasy romance author, language nerd and cartography enthusiast. Having grown up on a steady diet of epic fantasy, regency romance and cosy mysteries, she now writes steamy, swoony stories with a generous sprinkle of murder.

Lisette lives in the Netherlands (yes, below sea level) with her boyfriend and the few house plants that miraculously survive her highly irregular watering regime. When she's not reading or writing, she can usually be found drawing fantasy maps, baking and eating too many chocolate cookies, or geeking out over Ancient Greek.

To get in touch, visit www.lisettemarshall.com, or follow @authorlisettemarshall on Instagram, where she spends way too much time looking at pretty book pictures.

Printed in Great Britain
by Amazon

85692625R00174